HARD AND WARM
HIS BODY WAS...

his heart laboring under her ear, as he took her closely into his arms. His hands, grasping her head, pressed her hair up in a sort of crest, awkward and urgent, wildly tender. He drew her up from the bench, turned her face to his and kissed her mouth.

Sally broke from him and fled, crying, "No! I can't bear it! You hate me. I hate you. People think . . . people say . . ."

"Shut up, you little fool," he said roughly, and she stopped. "You know you're talking rot. I've been loving you ever since I first saw you. You know it. I've seen it in your eyes. Who cares what people say." And he took her once more into his strong, loving embrace. . . .

A Very Tender Love

by Katharine Newlin Burt

Originally titled Safe Road

A SIGNET BOOK
NEW AMERICAN LIBRARY
TIMES MIRROR

SIGNET TRADEMARK REG. U.S. PAT. OFF. AND FOREIGN COUNTRIES
REGISTERED TRADEMARK—MARCA REGISTRADA
HECHO EN CHICAGO, U.S.A.

SIGNET, SIGNET CLASSICS, MENTOR, PLUME AND MERIDIAN BOOKS
are published by The New American Library, Inc.,
1301 Avenue of the Americas, New York, New York 10019

FIRST PRINTING, SEPTEMBER, 1975

1 2 3 4 5 6 7 8 9

PRINTED IN THE UNITED STATES OF AMERICA

*"Pausing to throw backward a last view o'er
the safe road . . . 'twas gone."*
—ROBERT BROWNING.

Chapter 1

Caleb Winter died in anger, his last conscious act being one of punishment.

His little old lawyer, Joseph Marr, half pleased with secret information, trotted down the stairs of the immense old house that night with the look of a man who enjoys the sour flavor of a lemon drop. His cheeks were sucked in.

The woman he had known first as Caleb's housekeeper and for a matter of twelve years as Caleb's wife, stood under the high globe of light in the hall below, waiting for him. She had the shape and the expression of a woman who has waited long and well. Her blunt flat surfaces suggested the brush work of a modern painter who has chosen his subject rather for varied bulk than for gracefulness. In her dark silk dress, she stood, block-still, all her shadows pointing to the floor so that her eyes were blots under her brows, her mouth a black triangle beneath her nostrils. Her feet sent down strong roots of shadow as though to find earth beneath the ancient, polished boards. She watched Marr's descent, lowering her chin a trifle at each step. At the bottom she came closer and set her hand against the rail. She spoke to him in a voice as full as usual.

"Did you see the doctor upstairs? Did he tell you how long it would be?"

"He says your husband won't last till morning, Mrs. Winter."

"Then," she said presently, "would you kindly send off a wire for me in the village?"

Marr agreed with a wordless nod, rubbing his chin. He thought, "Better wait for the hatching of those chicks before you telegraph your count of them."

7

Isabella Winter stepped, with the tread of a woman noticeably wider in the hips than in the shoulders, into a side room where Marr could see her short stout body gleaming roundly as it bent over a desk. The room had been her office as housekeeper before and after her marriage to the wealthy New Englander to whom this Virginian estate had come by inheritance from his first wife, Jessica Crewe. Marr had seen the first Mrs. Winter bend over that same desk. "Racy long bones," he thought, "don't wear so well. This woman, now, has plenty of vigor, can take punishment, stand up under it."

He listened to the heavy rain outside. A night of spring, more fit for birth, he thought, than death. Caleb would not live to hear the last drops of that raining.

Isabella came out and handed him a paper. He noticed that her face was deeply flushed, even her eyes were shot with blood. He thought that she had taken an unconscionable time to write so brief a message.

"Caleb Winter dying. Come home. Will send chauffeur and car to meet you St. Charles Hotel Baltimore on Friday." It was addressed to Miss Sara Lee Keyne—a name unknown to Marr—at St. Sylvester's School in a town of Maryland.

Miss Mary Culpepper, head mistress of St. Sylvester's, kept an old-fashioned school for the new-fashioned daughters of re-fashioned parents. There she taught to eight hundred maidens a philosophy and a ceremonial which, in their homes and during their vacations, they saw, if not altogether discarded, certainly either ignored or exposed to ruthless and destructive criticism. The effect upon their personalities was, for the most part, an attitude of poise ... as that of a mast held straight between contrary winds. Those of them who were intelligent, arriving consciously; those who were merely instinctive, unconsciously ... at the conclusion that life, as it is lived, must be a matter of perpetual adjustment, of alert compromise, of continual selection, a voyage requiring the greatest nicety of personal pilotage.

Miss Culpepper herself was what so few women contrive to be—a pragmatic idealist: that is, she was neither fanatic nor sceptic. She was not unprepared for ecstasy but well armed against all necessary disillusionments: a small grey-haired, narrow-waisted woman, so long an example of erectness and correctness in posture and in speech that she had acquired the grace of a quill feather and the spontaneous precision of a Phœbe bird.

Said Mary Culpepper to her graduation class at a private five o'clock meeting in May over teacups and small cakes in her charming upstairs sitting room: "There is an expression—a little homely ... I shan't use it on graduation day ... but it's descriptive ... 'The world is your oyster.' Which means, I take it, that for such lucky young people as yourselves, there won't be much difficulty in prying open shells." She walked up and down the room, having instructed them to remain seated in various chintz-covered chairs and sofas and pleasantly sun-filled window seats. Her hands were behind her back ... an admirable little marching figure.

"I'd like you to remember that the first man to open an oyster was in search of food. The discovery of pearls must have been, and always will remain, a sort of happy accident. Children," here she tried not to speak too pointedly to a girl with tawny hair and enormous eyes who was listening as though created out of hunger and thirst for all the possible contents of a crustacean world, "I want you to open your oysters with an eye to nourishment." They all opened their eyes upon her as though she were a pearl. "Don't expect miracles ... raptures. Don't look for demigods to adore or to be adored by. Don't, for pity's sake, envisage yourselves as young princesses in towers or sirens upon rocks. Be women; and please try to know and to like *men* ... as you'll find them ... not the heroes and the demons of romance that the dream makers and reverie-producers tell you about. Learn to stand on your own two feet and keep those feet on the ground. Don't look about for masculine sofa cushions, not only material, but spiritual and mental ones." (Here Jenny Ainsworth smiled shyly at Martha Cramm, meaning to say, "What's *she* know about men?") "Try to get most of your experience first hand," said Miss Culpepper who had seen the smile, "and do, for the credit of St. Sylvester's, learn to enjoy yourselves. The phrase used to mean something. It might pay you to think it into its original freshness of imagery. That's a good trick if you want to savor your mother tongue. Enjoy *yourselves* without undue dependence upon others. Don't you come back to see me, five, ten, twenty years from now with that down-in-the-mouth, wan, blasted look I get on the faces of so many older women."

The girls laughed. One of them said in the voice of the eternal graduate, "Oh, *we* won't, Miss Culpepper!" and another, "We'll use make-up . . . if the worst comes to the worst, Miss Culpepper."

"I'd like you to have courage . . ." here she did allow herself a long and gentle look into the enormous eyes of the tawny-headed child, "and a philosophy for happiness, or for a reasonable enjoyment of reality, that, in its essentials, cannot altogether be taken from you by any man or child or other woman in the world. I don't," said Miss Culpepper, "admire unhappy women."

This was a dark saying. "But, Miss Culpepper, if things go wrong?"

"Things will go wrong, Emily. If things went right, there would be no need either for courage or philosophy."

Miss Culpepper kept one of the girls as the rest were leaving.

"Sally Keyne . . . come back a moment, please."

Sally exchanged a reassuring look with her disappointed roommate, Jane, closed the door on that familiar smooth departing back and turned into the room. The western light shone on her tawny hair and her enormous eyes blazed into green smiling.

Miss Culpepper smiled back and went over to sit before a small informal desk beside the window.

"I have a message for you, Sally. It came yesterday. From Mrs. Winter. I kept it until the examination was over. I cashed your last check for you and I have arranged for Miss Jenks to take you as far as the hotel in Baltimore." She took up a telegram and read aloud. "It says: 'Caleb Winter dying. Come home. Will send chauffeur and car to meet you St. Charles Hotel, Baltimore, on Friday.'" Immediately after reading, she handed it to Sally Keyne.

Under her lowered lashes the girl's bright eyes moved back and forth, her lips pressed themselves together.

"Come home ..." she repeated and looked up at Miss Culpepper. "That's funny, don't you think?"

"Don't be bitter, darling."

"Oh, I won't. Mother couldn't help it. If you marry a queer old man for his money, I suppose it's up to you to humor him. And ... being left with you was luck for me, wasn't it? But, Miss Mary, if I don't find it comfortable down there, may I come ... *home?*"

Miss Mary put up her hand but the girl, with a curiously maternal gesture, drew the grey head of her school mistress against her own side and pressed it there. The head was curiously submissive as though it craved protection. But, after an instant, its owner withdrew it and looked up into Sally's face.

"You must come back soon and often but I do want you to make a go of it down there in Virginia."

Sally walked over to a window and stood, her eyes widely open, staring at a rayless sun about to be brushed out by a green meadow horizon.

"I'm excited," she said. "It will be something happening to me ... myself ... not like visiting, watching other girls."

"You're older than the others ... nineteen. You'd have graduated two years ago ... if your life had been like theirs. You are really more ready for happenings than most of my graduates. It seems to me that you will find adventure everywhere. Only, at first, try to think most of your mother. This must have been cruel for her ... keeping you away. Waiting, perhaps, for a release."

Sally turned back from the window. Her very fair-skinned face showed two or three golden freckles like splashes of honey, because the color had dropped out of it.

"Miss Mary, you don't honestly know the first thing about ... me, do you? I mean, why I had to be this guilty secret?"

"Not guilty, Sally. I never suspected your mother of guilty secrecy. She told me only when she brought you here that her employer was a crotchety man and would give this excellent position only to a woman without family ties. He had no use for children. Later, after her marriage, she said that he would be jealous and very angry with the long deception she had practiced. She could not have you home ... explaining so belatedly the fact of your existence. She didn't ... for your sake ... dare to risk the exposure. So, you see, she has waited. Perhaps she knew it wouldn't be for long."

Sally's face, alternately unusually mobile or unusually tranced, now twisted itself wholeheartedly into a grimace that could not possibly be described by any word so harmless as a pout. It was a fierce young boyish scowl of mouth and brows and eyes.

"He must be a horrible man," she said and then amazement wiped away the scowl on a tide of rose-colored blood. "Must ... *have been.*" She flung herself across the room, her thin body with conspicuous firm young breasts moving with the fluency of water. "I must tell Jane! When do I go? What train? What train, Miss Mary?"

She caught herself at the door and made her face turn back. The eyes were golden, danced.

"On the six-thirty. But, Sally, wait a moment, dear. Can you wait ... listen to me a little longer?"

"Of course." The child sat down at once, submissively, surrendering her patient young attention.

"I suppose you and the other girls—I saw Jenny Ainsworth smiling when I talked about men!—think it funny sometimes for me to try to teach you about life and men and women, don't you? I mean, when I've been so shut in, so cloistered in a way, myself. Well, it's always interested me that through history the men and women behind walls, monks and priests, nuns and spinsters, have been preparing the adventurers for life. I can't explain that, nor justify it. It may have been a great misfortune, except for one fact ... the value of detachment. Adventurers are often too active to see the forest for its trees. We students keep ourselves apart and manage, for all our narrowness, sometimes, to keep in view the permanent, the universal values."

Sally's face wore now the quiet shadow of the cloisters; it had become the face of the disciple and the dreamer.

"I don't believe," she said very gravely, "that what

people say to you or teach to you counts such an awful lot, Miss Mary. I think it's what they are. I mean, I'm always listening to what you are. I've been about, you see, visiting. I must be the world's *most* visitor! All my holidays have been spent in other girls' homes, and I've had a chance to watch a lot of different sorts of people acting," said Sally, and added wryly, "Very often acting *up*. And I've had a chance to test you out, Miss Mary."

Miss Mary flushed, lifted her eyes in suspense to this girl's face which had, at times, the ruthlessness of a bare blade.

"You are so well equipped," Sally said, "for living, Miss Mary, that you could afford to give it up. It's like not calling on the pupils you know will be prepared."

Miss Mary laughed. "That's absolutely the best reward I've ever had, Sally." She waited for a minute thoughtfully and the girl waited, amazingly patient. "Tell me ... I don't want to hurt you, only help ... how do you feel about your mother?"

"I'm sorry for her more than anything else. She must have been afraid. Now, I'm hoping ..."

"Now, I think she will be free to do wonderful things for herself and for you. Caleb Winter is, or was, a very wealthy man. Your mother has been able to give you everything here, besides a liberal allowance. That proves that he was generous enough to allow her an unquestioned and secret expenditure."

"I don't like being a secret, especially an expensive one!"

"Of course you don't. That's over now. You can step out in the open, Sally, on a safe road."

Sally rose thoughtfully. "I think the safe road is back of me, Miss Mary." Her face kindled. "I shan't mind. I rather like the prospect of a little danger ... on ahead."

Chapter 2

For a tawny-haired adventurer of nineteen summers, Miss Amy Jenks, teacher of mathematics, was perhaps an uninspiring cicerone. She was that rare bird, a female mathematical genius, born counting her fingers and toes and immediately aware that little stars twinkle-twinkle of cosmic measurements. Miss Jenks, though by a further and even rarer gift she was actually able to move her pupils to excitement over a subject usually anathema to them, was perpetually disappointed by their abrupt loss of interest when they were released from the incandescence of her number-enchanted eye.

Miss Jenks was eager for disciples, even for one disciple, and ever and anon, fancying she had discovered one, her heart was broken by apostasy. She had for a few school periods entertained hopes concerning Sara Lee Keyne—a fantasy based upon the size and spiritual hunger of those eyes—but this illusion had long since vanished. She knew, when she asked Miss Culpepper if she might chaperone Sally as far as Baltimore because she had a sister there, that the journey would be for her intellectually a dead loss. Sally would use her great eyes for looking out of the window or at a magazine or her fellow travellers. Her attention to Miss Jenks' comments as to the extraordinary examples of relativity exhibited in walking down the aisle of a moving train which at the same moment was overtaking another train going in the same direction ... would be almost entirely perfunctory.

They arrived in Baltimore, however, in good and amiable spirits and Sally in her erect exclamatory writing, asking Miss Jenks first if she should do so, entered

14

their names on the hotel register. A neat, fresh-cheeked gentleman in pince-nez stood at her elbow politely postponing his own registration and also politely amused by hers. Sally then chose a large expensive double room overlooking the street. During these negotiations, Miss Jenks telephoned to her sister.

When she again achieved conjunction with her charge, Sally was enjoying the unique delight of spreading out a few toilet articles and some odd bits of clothing in the vast spaces provided. Turning at her chaperone's entrance she saw at once that Miss Jenks was abnormally in touch with disturbing and imminent realities. Her hat had gone very far back on her ginger-colored head.

"Oh, Sally, I don't know what to do!"

"What's wrong, Miss Jenks?"

Miss Jenks sat down on a chair immediately beside the bedroom door and played piano keys along the top of her handbag.

"Oh, I've been talking to my sister and she has to leave for Texas the first thing tomorrow. Her husband's got a job there. And she's rented her house and is in a room with just one extra sort of day bed. And we've only got this one evening for each other, maybe for years."

"Well," said Sally in her open and flexible young voice, "do please go right along and stay with her. I'm all right."

Miss Jenks' face wrinkled like a frost-bitten sickle pear. "Leave you alone in the hotel, Sally?"

"I'll be perfectly safe up here."

"Will you promise to keep the door locked?"

"It locks itself you know, Miss Jenks."

"And will you take your dinner in your room?"

This was disappointing, but then there is a certain aristocratic grandeur in the idea. Sally first flushed and then said, "O.K."

"Please not that expression, dear!"

"I will if you like, Miss Jenks."

The chaperone hesitated. "And your breakfast? You won't leave the hotel until the chauffeur calls for you?"

"There was a message for me at the desk. He'll be calling for me at nine o'clock tomorrow morning.

Please don't worry. Remember I'm not a pupil any more. St. Sylvester is through with his responsibility to me."

"But I was supposed to deliver you into the hands of your mother's chauffeur."

She laughed in a key too explosive for the proprieties, perhaps, but pleasantly contagious. She kissed Miss Jenks and urged her out of the door.

"I'll run in tomorrow morning early," said Miss Jenks, throwing a sop to conscience. "Be very careful, dear." She was walking out sidelong and really, with her funny squashed face and protruding eyes, looked something like a crab. "And you are a very sweet child, Sally. Good-bye, my dear, good night."

When she had gone, Sally, for that young joy in being on one's own, surrendered her body to an imaginary partner with whom she swooned out a few bars of a waltz, then threw herself down on one of the walnut imitation beds on her face with her hair hanging over her nose at one edge and her exquisite silken legs waving up at the other. Feeling, however, that for an aristocratic traveller about to order dinner in her own apartment, the attitude might not be appropriate, she rose and went back to the triple mirror before which she very seriously and even sadly brushed her dense short hair. Now she was feeling the wound of her parting with Miss Mary, and that sensation of stifled sweetness and unacknowledged fear that stood in her emotional lexicon for the image of her mother. And she was wondering with rapid heart what it would be like ... that home which she had never seen.

With no apparent connection she then, suffering an abrupt change of mood and subject, her face coming out of its tranced and cloistered pallor, remembered that downstairs, opening from the lobby, there had been a dress shop beside the door of which had been displayed a most exquisite evening gown of glacial-water green. This green exactly matched a pair of earrings her mother had given her for Christmas. "Mr. Winter," Isabella had written, using for Sally as always her husband's formal title, "gave me a whole boxful of jewelry. It belonged to his first wife and I don't like to wear any of it. Nor do I think he would like to see me in it. Certainly these beautiful green things would not be appropriate. So I am sending them to you, dearest baby, for they are honestly my own to do just what I like with and I like to think of you with your white skin and lovely yellow hair wearing the emeralds in your cunning little ears."

Sally had not yet worn the emerald earrings—they were far too extravagant for the evening uniforms at school—but with this dress they would be simply divine. She got out her purse, which was red to match her hat and the false carnation in her tweed buttonhole, and counted her cash. Sixty-five dollars. And the hotel room, dinner, breakfast, tips, couldn't possibly be more than $20.00. Well, the dress looked about $125.00 but these hotel shops sometimes had variable prices. Sally put on the red hat, got into the tweed jacket, took up her purse, gloves dangling elegantly through its strap, and, dropping her room key in her pocket, went down to the dress shop. She would keep her promise not to go out alone into the street, although it was a lovely warm May evening and a quick walk after the stuffy train ride would be restful; also there was a good picture running at The Venetia; but, certainly, she could and would go about a bit inside the hotel. No one could object to that.

The dress was only $50.00. It fitted her divinely, slim as a grass snake she looked and white of skin as a wood-anemone of petals. And she was taller in it, or would be when she wore her silver slippers, than in any dress she'd ever worn before. Sally managed, with all the earnestness and sorrow of young eyes, to convince the saleswoman that she hadn't a cent more than forty to spend but that for forty this would be a definite sale. So that after consultation with Madame, who had an Irish accent, behind a screen, the dress was "practically given away."

It would be sent up to Miss Keyne in Room 825 as soon as the shoulder strap had been adjusted and the pressing done. Sally got back into her slim tweeds, bought two magazines and a box of cigarettes and sat in a tapestry and oaken throne to watch, for a few ecstatic minutes, the entrances and exists of the lobby.

She discovered that tonight in the hotel there was going to be a ball.

Dinner, served by a grave waiter in her own room, was magnificent but, for a girl newly released into her own life and vibrant with anticipation, a trifle desolate. After it, she smoked a cigarette ... smoking had been forbidden by St. Sylvester ... and then tried on her dress. After she had put on the earrings and sleeked back her hair, allowing it to curl forward under the decorated ears, and had wondered whether the back wasn't a bit too conspicuous by its absence, she stood at her window looking at the pretty lights of Baltimore. The sound of music moved her. There was that ball being given for some lucky Baltimore girl downstairs. The lobby and the cocktail bar would be filled with girls and boys in evening dress. She wouldn't be at all conspicuous, she could wear the silver jacket, rabbit-trimmed, that went with the new dress. She would go down and just look on at the dislocated fragments of the festivities. Before her mirror she arranged a pose of glacial dignity which lasted until she had placed herself in one of the least conspicuous lobby thrones where she forgot it because of pleasure in her colorful surroundings. She even forgot to smoke, just sat with enormous waltzing eyes, her tawny head drawn up and back, more decorative to the lobby than she could possibly have imagined. The Sally that showed herself in mirrors was never the Sally that looked out upon the world.

A man came round her pillar and spoke to her.

"Miss Keyne?"

She looked up at him, immediately relieved to find him ruddy, elderly, and wearing pince-nez.

"May I stand here and chat with you a moment? Until your friends arrive? I know the lady you are travelling with ... Miss Jenks."

"Oh, do you? She's gone to her sister's. Do you know Mrs. Caspar too?"

"Yes, indeed."

"Her husband has just got a job in Texas."

"Glad to hear it. An excellent opening. I'm glad you got your pretty dress, Miss Keyne. It was brought to me by mistake. Your 825 looked like 625. Luckily I'm an honest man."

Sally could think then of nothing more to say and wished that he would leave her. She remembered now that he had been standing at her elbow when she asked Miss Jenks if it would be all right for her to register their names. Being decently polite to him now was a nuisance, distracted her from happy observation of the excited arrivals and the cocktail-seekers of the ball. And yet, in a way, it was pleasant not to sit there quite alone.

Watching her eyes, her self-introduced companion said, "How about a cocktail?"

Sally answered "I'd love one," before she thought, "Maybe I oughtn't to. Oh well, he does know Miss Jenks and Mrs. Caspar!"

"I had to promise not to go out of the hotel," she told him, seated at a small table in the gay Hispano-Baltimore bar. "So I'm lucky that there's so much going on inside tonight."

"I consider myself the lucky one. A menthe frappé?"

"Yes, Mr. . . . I don't know your name."

"Hinckel. Maybe Miss Jenks . . ."

"Miss Jenks hardly ever talks about people. Her mind is very, very abstract, don't you think?"

"Extremely," said Mr. Hinckel, who had, Sally thought, a rather abstract manner himself. Or was it just that he was concentrating on something or somebody . . . she felt a sort of glow and tingle of unpleasant discovery . . . upon herself? This idea, once suggested, became more and more confirmed. She drank her frappé and wondered wretchedly whether the fact that his knees kept pressing against hers under the table was accidental. Didn't he have any sensation in his old legs?

"I shall have to go up to my room now, Mr. Hinckel. You've been ever so kind but I've had such a long day."

"What about your friends?"

Sally kept herself from telling him that she had no expectation of friends or escorts, that she had put on an evening dress merely . . . rather according to Miss Culpepper's recommendation . . . to enjoy *herself*. He might think she had been sitting in the lobby waiting to be picked up.

"Don't tell me you're tired. I never saw anyone look fresher. But your cheeks are getting very pink. Maybe it's too hot for you in here. Let me take you for a run. My car is just outside."

"Oh no, indeed, thank you very much. I promised Miss Jenks."

"When is she coming back?"

"Not until tomorrow morning just before I leave."

Sally had got herself out into the lobby again and was threading her way amongst the black tails and the rainbow chiffon-trails. She was beginning to feel very uneasy now with Mr. Hinckel so close and so protective, holding her elbow very definitely in his hand.

He was evidently determined to steer her out through the revolving door, and poor Sally foresaw a most uncomfortable scene. He couldn't force her to go for a ride in his car but he was counting on her young timidity, her fear of being rude to an older man, of making a mistake, a conspicuous fool of herself.

"Your young man," said Mr. Hinckel in a tone of false sympathy, "must have forgotten you."

A group of people were preventing their advance by turning like so much bright grist through the mill of the revolving doors. One of these, a young fellow in "tails," with a high dark curly head, paused just inside, alone, to light a cigarette.

"Oh, there," cried Sally, "there he is. Thank you so much, Mr. Hinckel. Good night." She jerked her elbow free, moved rapidly over to her selected rescuer and holding him, almost in Mr. Hinckel's fashion, by the elbow, said with what remained of her scared breath, "Oh, please look as if you knew me. Smile! I'm alone in the hotel and I'm being bothered by . . . a man."

"Why, hul-lo!" cried the young man with a flashing smile, grabbing her hand. "It's you, is it? At last!"

"I'm so terribly grateful to you," Sally murmured, almost in tears. "I didn't know what to do. I want the man to think that I'm going to this party. Would it be too awful to ask you to take me in and dance just half a dance with me? I won't be . . . a nuisance. Honestly. You can take me right out by another door and put me into an elevator somewhere. I'm staying in the hotel. I . . . I'm really not this kind of girl."

He was looking down at her through criss-cross eye-lashes.

"I saw you the second I came in," he said moving cordially with his attractive narrow head bent towards her like a most devoted escort's. "That's why I stopped to light a cigarette. I wanted to get another look at you. I was hoping you'd be at the dance. I thought the old boy was your father."

Sally laughed and told herself, "I do laugh too loud. Miss Mary's right. This boy doesn't like me laughing so loud."

"I wondered," he was going on with unchanged cheerfulness, however, "why you looked so pink and worried."

"Did I?"

"You did. I thought it might be just deb-fever, before a ball, you know. Don't worry. I'm crashing the party myself. I came along with a friend of mine ... the big Swede ahead with a girl in a red dress. He's going on to another party afterwards. I think he knows the hostess here. I don't. The party is being given for a gal named Martha. That's as far as I go. Come on. We'll crash together. Good music. My name is Robin Ashe. From Yale via Virginia."

They danced out upon a perfect floor. Sally was thinking that if she had stopped to look him over first she would never have had the nerve to pick this boy up at all. For he was a correct young gentleman. His face and carriage had what Sally was in the habit of calling "that inherited look"—eyes dark, bright, ironic in the attractive narrow head, a mouth and chin evidently handed down to him by a serenely beautiful mother. He had just the right clothes, she felt sure, and just the right manner for any occasion, even for this one of being picked up by a strange girl.

As a result of these observations, she made haste to give him her credentials, such as they were.

"My name is Sara Keyne. I'm ... St. Sylvester's."

"Really? I've got a kid cousin there. Patty May."

"I know her well. I helped to initiate her. What year are you at Yale?"

"Junior. I'm in the architectural school."

"Then you might know Ollie Mortimer."

"Do I know Ollie! He's the roommate of one of my best friends."

"Oh, Mr. Ashe, he's my roommate's ... it's not exactly out yet ... fiancé. Maybe Ollie has spoken to you about her. Jane Trimble?"

"I have faced Jane's photograph for two long wistful years."

"Isn't this funny?"

"Oh, I don't know. People of the same kind do gang up on each other. That's what one of our old colored men says about wasps, they gang up on him. Not that we are wasps, you're not anyway. More like a be-autiful katydid. Oh, no, please, not by that door," for Sally had selected her exit. "You can go round a few more times. Look, Miss Keyne, I have good ideas sometimes; you'd be surprised! I can introduce you to Billy and he can pretend he brought you and take you up to make your curtsey to whoever our hostess is. Then you'll have your pass and we can dance it out. I'll give up Bill's second party."

"I can't really. I wouldn't like to do that."

"Forget good old Sylvester! We are practically childhood friends. I won't let you do the Cinderella act. I like the way you dance and the way you talk. I like what you have on and the way you do your hair."

"I don't do it."

"That's why it looks so pretty."

"I *am* having fun," she said.

They danced for a little while in silence.

"As a rule," he said, "I don't like these big nameless parties but this is going to be very, very different."

"Really I can't stay, Mr. Ashe. Please take me out by *that* door."

"All right." Robin smiled slyly and beyond the door she found herself in a room with palms and small tables and rosy lights. There they sat down, close and opposite, and he captured her a cold drink.

"A mild punch," he assured her. "Don't balk."

He lighted her a cigarette.

"Where do you go from here, Miss Keyne?"

"You mean?"

"Back to St. Sylvester's or home for a spring vacation?"

"Tomorrow I'm going down to my home for good. A place in Virginia. My mother's name is Mrs. Caleb Winter. She ... lives in ... I mean ... my home is ... the old Crewe place not very far from Jamestown."

"*The* Crewe place? That's one of the most famous plantations in Virginia. I was taken over it once on a visiting day." He looked at her now with a new expression and for the first time Miss Mary's ward, used to a position anomalous and humiliating, tasted that small sweet flavor of a worldly pride. She knew that she was of importance socially and remembered that Caleb Winter had been a very wealthy man.

It was apparent, too, that the attitude of her escort had indefinably changed. Cinderella's dress and slippers began to be of a real-princess quality.

"You know," he was saying more gravely than he had yet spoken, "my place isn't so far away." Then he smiled in a sly sweet fashion inherited too, she fancied, from the beautiful mother, "within easy motoring distance. I bet you ride to hounds ..."

"I have never hunted. But I've ridden quite a lot. I haven't been home," she turned away her eyes, she simply could not bring herself to say "ever," "such a lot. My ... my stepfather has been ill."

She wondered if this boy knew something about the peculiarities of Caleb Winter, for he gave her an enigmatic look, compounded of sympathy and a certain cynicism. He stood up.

"Let's crash another dance." He whistled music. "I like this tune."

"No, really. I'm ... tired."

"Will you go out with me then, for just a little run before you turn in?"

"All right," said Sally, eager to escape an introduction under false colors, and she went across the lobby and, this time, out through the revolving doors. Mr. Hinckel was in the cocktail bar. She saw him drinking beside a woman in a street suit and a smart black hat.

"Wait here a sec," Robin told her on the step. "I'll bring round the machine."

She stood there in front of the hotel. The street was crowded and a late limousine parked almost in front of the steps was causing trouble. The doorman was abusing its driver, a nonchalant fellow in a smart uniform. One of those interminable masculine open air tongue battles was going on, the big doorman and another man in hotel uniform arguing with the imperturbable chauffeur. "All right. All right. Don't lose your fancy shirt. Give me a sec, I'm pulling out." But, as he moved his gears, a third figure, shabby, active, urgent, sprang up the step, thrusting aside the doorman.

"Hi, you George!"

"Hullo, is that you, Vincent?"

"Sure it's me. Give me a lift tomorrow, will you? I got to beat it down your way."

"Lost your job?"

"Kicked out of the St. Charles garage after twenty-four hours of perfect soivice. That's what I was."

The doorman took hold of him roughly by the shoulder.

"Get out of here, will you? Don't you see this car is blocking the way?"

At the touch, "Vincent" whirled like a wildcat, showing an unshaven glittering sort of face, copper red under the street light. There was a savage scuffle during which the dismissed mechanic was thrust against Sally. He looked up at her and would, from the changed expression of his hard blue eyes, have apologized if she, thinking of her new dress, had not drawn it quickly away. The gesture was in the melodramatic tradition of the contemptuous aristocrat.

"It won't hurt you to get bumped by one of the unemployed, lady," said the offender.

And at this instant Robin Ashe returned, saw Sally's startled face and angry eyes—angry in fact, rather for the man's accusation of class-contempt than for his insolence; saw the scowling, unshaven face of her accoster and, with no hesitation whatever, drove a hard athlete's fist into his mouth. The man went down and the hotel servants sprang to prevent an instantaneous resurrection. "Oh, please, please," cried Sally.

"Better go along with her right away, sir," suggested the panting doorman. "We can take care of him, don't you worry."

Sally threw herself, with one of those light practiced movements of machine-accustomed youth, into the car—during the scuffle George in the handsome limousine had driven silently away—but there, an instant later, her conscience came awake.

"I'm breaking my promise to Miss Jenks," she told Ashe unevenly for the fight on the step had shaken her nerves. "I've never broken a promise in my life. You've got to take me once round the block and back."

"Twice," begged Robin. "Three times."

On the second return he mournfully agreed to take her to the elevator, but followed her therein and stepped out with her on the eighth floor.

"You really do live at the Crewe place, don't you?" he asked her before 825 in a voice of nervous tension. "You are really a neighbor? You're not going to do anything as low as to vanish out of my life tomorrow?"

"If anyone vanishes it will be you, Robin Ashe. I'll be at the Crewe House all the rest of my life probably. If you are really only thirty miles away, vanishing and reappearing is definitely up to you."

"Definitely," said Robin. He paused. "Sally . . . a . . . a kiss?"

His voice close to her ear was not steady, had no insolence.

The corridor of the eighth floor of the St. Charles seemed very still. Sally looked at him beautifully with all her eyes. She was serious and pale.

"I think not, Robin . . . please."

"Just as you say."

He waited. Was it possible, thought Sally, that she could hear the beating of his heart?

"Good night. Thanks awfully." She smiled and gave him her hand.

He hurt it. She opened the door, went in, smiled again with her eyes lowered away from the look that had come into his, before she shut him out.

She heard the clashing of the elevator doors and the sound of its descent.

It wasn't his heart at all, for pity's sake! It was her own. Sally Keyne's heart! How perfectly ridiculous!

Chapter 3

The chauffeur sent up word promptly at nine o'clock that he was ready to start whenever Miss Keyne wished. He would come up for the bags. While he was carrying them out, Sally received a farewell visit from Miss Jenks, who thus technically fulfilled the terms of her obligation to deliver Sally into the hands of the chauffeur. Miss Jenks was full of her sister's emergencies, giving Sally just one observant glance. "You look a mite tired, dear," she exclaimed; "didn't you sleep well?" but went on at once without waiting for an answer.

In Caleb Winter's limousine Sally set out upon the second stage of her journey, which seemed to her indeed to be the first steps upon that new road whose safety Miss Culpepper had so confidently predicted. Sally was still child enough to be busy at first in examining the detail of her conveyance: the soft folded rug, the charming little clock, the vase, the calendar, the memorandum book with its pencil, the cigarette lighter and ash tray, the mouthpiece for orders to the chauffeur. She had presently a use for this. Caleb Winter's man pulled up at a gas station only a few blocks from the hotel where, to her astonishment, he took on a front-seat passenger, a young fellow hatless and in overalls who mounted quickly, grinning up at the chauffeur and throwing not so much as a glance at Sally in her handsome enclosure. She took up the mouthpiece.

"Chauffeur."

"Yes, miss," the tone was somewhat startled.

"Who just climbed in?"

"Er ... it's a friend of my own, Miss Keyne. I'm

giving him a lift, if you please, miss." This he added as by an afterthought.

At that instant "the friend" turned his broad shoulder in its faded khaki shirt and looked back at her through the glass. He was deeply sunburnt so that a strip of skin white as a bandage showed under his recently cropped hair. He had been shaved and she might not have recognized him if it had not been for a puffy cut at the corner of his heavily lipped mouth. His eyes were slate blue, surly and cold.

"George," said Sally, "that *is* your name, isn't it?" The blood was pounding into her cheeks. "I'm sorry. I can't let you give this man a lift. I don't think Mrs. Winter would approve."

For a bewildered second she thought the man would defy her orders but he said reluctantly, "Very well, Miss Keyne," and turned to his companion.

The two men exchanged a few emphatic remarks, inaudible to Sally, and a sort of insolent shrug. The younger one, whose face had deepened to a copper color, then flung Sally another look, uglier than the first, and climbed down. To her amazement he coolly opened her own door.

"I wish you a pleasant journey, lady," he said, in a voice drawling and soft, "and an exclusive one. You are sure enough going to take up more than your fair share of space in a mightily crowded world."

He grinned, the hard grin of an angry man, and shut the door emphatically.

"Go on, George, at once," cried Sally into her mouthpiece.

A few miles further forward, George stopped and in his turn came around to her door. His cap was in his hand.

"I'm sorry, Miss Keyne. I wouldn't have caused you trouble but, you see, it's like this. From the way Mrs. Winter spoke I kind of thought you'd be a little girl like. So last night I gave this chap my word."

"Yes," said Sally, "I was there in front of the hotel while you were giving it. You didn't let me know that you had arrived last night. I suppose that was because you thought I'd had an early supper and been put—to bed. Is this 'Vincent' an old friend of yours?"

George wore his own shade of red, more salmon than copper.

"Well no, miss, I can't say so. I sort of fell into acquaintance with him in the hotel garage. He, in a manner of speaking, did me a favor. He seemed all right, miss, a cut above the usual mechanic."

"You see, George, it was a young man with me last night, who knocked him down in front of the St. Charles. That was just after you had driven away, I think, George. Shall we go on now?"

"Yes, miss," said the chauffeur with meekness.

It was not until they stopped for lunch in one of the quaint and wistful towns of Maryland, beginning to retire under its summer roof of green, that Sally bethought herself of an inquiry which, had it not been for the accident of Vincent's intrusion, she should have put before.

"George," she said in a somewhat faltering voice, standing beside him on the pavement in front of the small café, "I want to know about ... poor Mr. Winter."

"Good heavens, Miss Keyne. Didn't you get any message? Mr. Winter died on the Monday and the funeral took place on the Thursday. That would be yesterday at noon, miss."

Sally said nothing. She went in soberly and ate a sandwich and drank tomato juice. The news was expected and she could not feel regret. The death of an unknown Caleb Winter meant for her the opening of a door long cruelly locked against entrance into home and happiness.

When she came out to the car, "Tell me, George," she asked him before climbing in, "how is Mother?"

George said, "That would be Mrs. Winter?"

"Of course. Is she ... I mean, does she seem all right?"

"Oh, quite composed, miss. Bearing up wonderful."

In her padded glass cage Sally drew herself back and down into as small a compass as though she had in fact been the little girl George had expected, and suffered bitterly. "Mother should have explained me. She should have told George about me. Won't anyone know?" Tears, for all she could do to choke them, press them back, burst into her throat and eyes. Oh, what is wrong about me? What is the truth? That doubt which inevitably had stung her secret mind as to her legitimacy now cut her with a quick stripe of shame. She turned her face against the seat and called upon Miss Mary. It was astonishing how promptly that clear Phœbe-bird voice made answer. "I don't admire," Miss Mary said above the humming of the car, "unhappy women." Sally thought, "I'm really Mary Culpepper's daughter," and, sitting up, mopped her eyes, blew her nose, pulled on the hat misery had forced her to discard and, tightening her mouth, looked out with determined interest upon the scenery. Fortunately they were about to cross the wide exciting waters of the Chesapeake, a three-hour ferriage to Norfolk, and she had the beauty of sunset sky and water, of distant blossom-foaming shores, and of church spires and the harbor traffic to distract her from her hurt. She stood hatless upon the ferry deck under a strong warm wind, that smelled of river banks and river currents, stripping her face and neck of its bright mane ... to face Virginia. It was not her native state. She knew that she had been born in Ohio. But it was Robin's. She amused herself by humming against the wind, "What's this dull town to me, Robin's not here; What was't I wished to see, What wished to hear?" And it would, from this day forward, be her own. Crewe House, the great old plantation of Crewe! She felt a pang for this, its fate of inheritance by strangers. Were any of the Crewes alive to resent her mother's ownership? Caleb Winter's housekeeper, to be the successor of Jessica and all the old dead Crewes. And Caleb Winter's stepdaughter, this Sara Lee Keyne who now stood windstripped and shining like a figure on a Viking prow, to widen her enormous hungry eyes at that approaching soil. Sunset painted her and painted the water to a glow of pride, of welcome.

Darkness had fallen before George told her through her tube, "We're just turning into your mother's gate, Miss Keyne. It's a famous driveway and I'm sorry I couldn't have got you here while it was light."

Sally, peering forth, did see the lights of a great house ahead at the far end of some tall passage of invisible trees. The door had opened, a dark figure stood in outline. After two minutes, Sally ran up some shallow steps and, between two white pillars, was caught into a strong embrace and held against the longed for, unfamiliar but faithfully remembered breast of her strange mother.

Mrs. Winter kept repeating, "Sally . . . Sally . . ." and crying; until Sally laughed and said, "Do let's go in, Mother darling, where I can see you."

She soon looked away from her mother, who was changed. It was not that Isabella Winter wore the wan, down-in-the-mouth, blasted look of Miss Culpepper's accusation, but that her strong square face carried fierce scars of patience and a sombre light of its reward. Sally, who had the primitive gift of seeing her world in pictures, was reminded of a dark lantern, a light carried by a thief in secret under a stealthy cloak.

But the house was beautiful! She was bewildered by the great hall, its stairs sweeping upward as though with a life and grace of intention, and bearing, as her mother had written her, on its balustrade the scars of a British officer's sabre, when, drunk and startled by an alarm of rebels, he had ridden his horse up the wide steps to rouse his stupefied dragoons, and down again in a rage at their and perhaps at his own intoxication. The point of that angry sabre was still embedded in the newel post. To right and left of this central hall, which cut through from front to back, room after beautiful room tempted Sally's ecstatic exploration. "Mother, I didn't dream it would be so perfectly marvellous. The panelling and the portraits, and the wonderful old furniture. Flowers everywhere. Have we a greenhouse? And books, books, books; whole walls full of books. I shall get educated! And such splendiferous fireplaces. Is this the drawing room? Washington visited here? And Jefferson? Oh, look, two little staircases up to our second story."

"Sally darling, leave it until tomorrow." Mrs. Winter followed her, half scared by the clapping voice and footsteps of youth. "Dinner has been waiting for us. Just wash your face and hands down here in the dressing room. Ah, here is Charles now. Charles, this is my daughter."

Sally's gay excitement ended. She turned in a mood

of pride and suspicion and saw a tall old colored man, gray-headed, very soft and serious of expression, grand in a dinner coat, who made her a ducking bow and smiled like a toothless seraph. "We's proud to have you home, Miss Sally."

Sally felt quick color and hid quick tears. So she was not a stranger. She had been explained, accounted for. Turning, she flung her arms tightly around her startled mother.

In the handsome dining room, with its banqueting table and carved, high-backed chairs, its sideboards laden with old silver, its Crewe portraits looking down their long straight noses between their wigs or their auburn curls, Caleb Winter's widow and the daughter of whose very existence he had been ignorant, sat at a small breakfast table and ate admirable food, admirably served by Charles and a younger man.

Sally, whose tongue like her face was alternately mobile or trained, chattered constantly. The glory of her new home, the delight of her home-coming, had gone to her head, releasing her as wine does, from shyness and reserve. She told her mother graphically and with that too explosive laughter, the story of her Baltimore adventures. "Do you know Robin Ashe? Or anyone of that name?"

"I think so. A Mrs. Jaffery Ashe called here once on her way through. It was on one of the visiting days. They're rather a nuisance."

"But, Mother, it's such a beautiful, historic place people ought to be allowed to see it. All those exquisite things."

Mrs. Winter shrugged. "I ought to know it. It was my duty to show people about. Every chair and shelf and table and volume and knickknack I've had the care of now for twelve years. When I was Mr. Winter's housekeeper."

Sally then gave her a shy look. They had moved into one of the smaller drawing rooms for coffee and were alone. "Wasn't it sort of queer, Mother, I mean, changing from being his housekeeper to being his wife?"

"I'd been his only companion for so long, Sally. We were quite used to each other. I just . . . moved in."

She flushed for the first time, perhaps, in many years.

"I was very fond of my husband, Sally. He was a strange man, I know. Very solitary and didn't like people. He had an unfortunate habit of suspicion. He had been hurt and deceived ... terribly. And that led him to spying and inquiring and listening to tittle-tattle sometimes, so that he heard the unpleasant falsely colored reports that are so often carried to the ears they weren't properly tuned for."

"Mother." Sally was sitting against cushions in one of those graceful, impossible contortions of a very young girl and now she began to look down studiously at a figurine her fingers teased on the table behind their couch. Mrs. Winter could see the flushed fair cheek and the lamp-brightened hair, the tip of a straight short, rather wide-bridged nose and the sensitive movements of her lips in profile. "Did ... do you suppose he ever suspected about ... me?"

Mrs. Winter got up, walked stiffly away to another table, found a workbag there and came back, all without speech. "No," she said then.

She sat down upright, both feet on the floor, put horn-rimmed glasses on her nose and began to knit with short dark capable fingers.

"You're in deep mourning, aren't you, Mother? Should I wear black?"

"Certainly not. I want you to be the gayest and happiest girl in all Virginia. As soon as a decent time has passed, I shall try to give some parties for you. I've not gone about much but people know me here. They don't dislike me. They'll be glad to have Crewe House open again. It used to have famous hospitality."

Through the shelter of her fingers and her eyelashes, Sally wondered what sort of hostess for gay young parties this grave old woman, so plainly dressed and plainly spoken, would make. But the desire to love softened her naked young discernment. She slid forward and down at full length and put the weight of her silken shining head upon Mrs. Winter's knees. "I'm horribly sleepy," said Sally, "and horribly happy. These last two days have been the first real days of my life."

Her mother watched her to her high four-posted bed in a room fit, said Sally, for a "colonial angel." The poor woman savored with a starved pride this gazing over the bath-dampened, outspread hair, the drowsy green-grey-golden eyes and the fair, strong-boned, rose-mouthed face of her lost baby. The collar of Sally's schoolgirl pajamas stood up like a careless little boy's about her throat. Her mother smoothed it down. "You're lovely, my sweet Sally." Isabella Winter's mouth controlled a spasm. "You don't hate me, do you?"

"Hate you? Why, Mother!"

"You might ... fairly. I've given you a pretty raw deal. No home. No mother. No ... no love."

"Oh, but you have. I always knew you gave me that."

One of the square dark hands was now across Mrs. Winter's eyes, the other clenched in the blanket cover. "I do, Sally. I always have, indeed. I've loved you, thought of you ... most."

Sally came up from her covers like a rubber toy and on her knees hugged her mother, pressing down the black-grey head against her firm little breasts with that fierce maternal protectiveness, quaint to see in the figure of a fair-haired Pierrot. And, like Mary Culpepper's, the tired head of Caleb Winter's housekeeper submitted gratefully. It was good to be *mothered* after the bleak untender years.

Sally was waked late next morning by the arrival of a breakfast tray in the hands of a pretty mulatto girl.

"I'm Early, Miss Sally. Yas'm," she chuckled with Sally, though without quite knowing the cause of mirth. "Yas'm, I'm named Early. I'm Mr. Charles' cousin's sister's gal. I've been broken in to serve you, Miss Sally. Now you're to give me orders. Your trunk 'rived here las' evenin'. You got a li'l dressin' room for your self, with so many drawers and shelves as a bride. Sure enough, you goin' to be a proud li'l miss, ma'am."

Sally ate her breakfast and chatted, dressing afterwards with speed. "Is Mother up?" she asked.

"Sure. Your mother she ain't no layabed, murnin's." Early went sober. "Now she down with Mr. Marr, Miss Sally. It's the readin' of Mr. Winter's will, Miss Sally, ma'am. And they is shut away in Mis' Winter's work-an'-orderin' room. Best you not go a-pokin' round. They's awful solemn ... those last wills and ligaments."

Sally avoided the work-and-ordering room, going out quickly through the glass doors of the hall opposite her last night's entrance. Just outside she stopped. Tulips. White, yellow, scarlet, purple-black, a world of sunlit tulips. They nodded towards her. Beyond them ran the foam of dogwood trees and further she could see through lovely vistas the long green meadows with their dark groves going down with all the ancient dignity of meadows to the river. A stable roof suggested saddle horses and Sally with elevation of heart saw herself riding to hounds with Robin Ashe. She ran around the house, saw box hedges, tall and black as cliffs, saw an avenue of immense buttonwoods, smelled May roses and jasmine. A mocker sang, birds were lively everywhere.

Coming back into the house by its front door, she heard a bell ringing. It was being frantically pressed. She hurried past the closed door to the left and, after an instant of hesitation, mounted slowly up the stairs. Perhaps she had better keep to her own room until they called her. She was halfway up the first flight when a maid and a man came running out into the hall. The closed door popped open. A man's sharp, frightened voice bespoke them.

"Grace ... Henry ... what in Heaven's name has kept you? Couldn't you hear that bell? Come here quickly. You must help Mrs. Winter. She ... I fear ... she has been taken very ill."

Down the stairs Sally dropped with the unconscious speed of dreams, and saw her mother carried out by both servants, her head hanging, her face darkly distorted, unable, it seemed, to focus her bloodshot open eyes. Sally cried out to the little tight-faced gentleman who emerged just behind them, "What's the matter? Tell me, please, what's wrong? What did you do to make her look like this?"

The little man spoke tartly but with considerable sympathy, "It was the shock. I've sent for a doctor, Miss Keyne. Please to come down here as soon as you are able to leave your mother. I must have an urgent and important talk with you."

Chapter 4

That sour sweet flavor of secret information had become too sharp even for the acidic taste of Joseph Marr. The little old lawyer waited for Sally's return miserably enough, moving on his jerky thin legs across the ancient boards of the floor, from a sun-filled window to a closed door and back. This workroom of Caleb's former housekeeper had, for Marr, several ghosts but he now wished, even to brushing the recollection from his shaggy brows, that it had not been possessed by what he had just seen: this solid, steady woman pushing herself up from her chair, staggering woodenly to prop herself before him at the desk edge on both her broad strong hands. "Let me see the words," she had said thickly, "let me see Caleb's words." And, having seen them, she had slumped down to her knees, then to the floor.

Marr had been frightened, not so much by the loss of consciousness which even in this woman had not been unnatural, as by the dreadful flush on her forehead and the twisted aspect of her face. "It was a stroke, that's what it was!" and he clicked and clucked taking back his judgment as to the superior strength of bones not fined by "race." The woman had not been able after all to take her punishment. And just punishment, the stern old lawyer still considered it. Isabella Grove—yes, she'd given the name of Grove!—had come to Crewe House under false colors and had deceived her husband long and well. Evidently Caleb's belated suspicion was amply justified. There stood the child, or rather there, for one glittering instant, she had stood, looking, thought Marr, astonished by his own simile, like a tulip at a funeral.

35

Gad, it was hard, that law of innocence suffering for guilt. The girl had just been told to "come home." Marr remembered well enough the message and Isabella's heavy flush. That would have been evidence of high blood pressure, dangerously high, one of those unheeded warnings. "Caleb Winter dying. Come home," addressed to St. Sylvester's, a smart, expensive school. Isabella must secretly have spent a pretty penny. Brought up the girl to be an heiress, ready to step into Jessica's slippers and to dance her pretty way into Virginian county life.

Tchk! Tchk! No amount of clacking could steady his nerves against the impending interview. Joseph knew next to nothing about the reactions of a schoolgirl. This girl was an outspoken piece, had already dared to upbraid him, even without an introduction! "What have you done to my mother?" That was to be it, was it? Well, my girl, what I've got to give you will trounce the starch out of you. Tears! Oh, Lordy, Lordy. Why couldn't he send his clerk, Anthony Card, to handle this wretched piece of business? Marr had half decided to run away and to appoint his young assistant to dry the tears of Miss Sara Lee Keyne, when, to prevent him, came a step, a knock and to his rather feeble invitation, the entrance of the girl herself.

He had been thinking of her as a saucy minx, now he saw that she was a badly frightened child.

He took her hand and put her into a sofa and sat there beside her, keeping the hand, which she, however, smiling at him uncertainly, withdrew and caught tightly in the other.

"Tell me please," she said.

He was absolutely abashed by the greatness of her eyes. They were too close for composure. He stood up and began his trotting, an exercise that had stood him in good stead under other accusing or beseeching eyes, making of him a difficult target.

"How is Mrs. Winter?"

"The doctor is with her now. She ... I think she's conscious. She tried to tell me something."

The child's mouth had the pitiful sharp edges of young self-control.

"Well ... well ... well ... it's hard. It's pretty hard.

Yes. Yes. But I dare say she'll come round, be better almost at once. She has a sound constitution. And how are *you* fixed for courage, for good old-fashioned American grit, Miss Keyne?"

She shook back her tawny short mane. He found it a reassuring gesture.

"All right," he said. "We'll get right down to brass tacks, shall we? You can take it, I reckon. Caleb Winter has left his entire property, estate, house, etc., etc., to the nephew of his first wife, the son of her deceased and only brother. The heir is named Obadiah Crewe."

Sally "took it" without so much as a flicker. Her lips, unpainted, remained delicately rose.

"And nothing for my mother?"

"Yes." Marr trotted the full length of his patrol and back, bent over the papers on the desk as though for verification, even clamping on his glasses, quite as if he had needed to see the words.

"'To my second wife and former housekeeper, Isabella, called when she came into my service, Isabella Grove, I hereby bequeath the shelter of my roof during the remainder of her natural lifetime, and wages amounting to the sum of three hundred dollars a month, to be enjoyed by her during the aforesaid lifetime, on condition that she will faithfully and humbly remain in residence at Crewe House in the capacity of housekeeper and obedient to the orders of Obadiah Crewe, son of my deceased wife's brother, and, as such, my legal heir.' ... I knew, my dear young lady, that this would be a severe blow to Mrs. Winter's confident hopes and pride, but I had supposed her strong enough to receive it without more preparation than I did, believe me! endeavor to furnish before reading out this clause of my late client's will."

"She couldn't bear it," Sally whispered, "because of me."

Her eyes then filled with crystal ichor which stood in them without falling and painted for her, no doubt, a vague prismatic world.

"I dare say. I dare say. Well, I can only hope, my dear, that she has managed to lay by out of the liberality of her late husband during these past twelve years, capital enough to make you both independent of this, I must say, *ironic* offer. . . . To put it mildly!" snapped Mr. Marr, suddenly and to his own surprise, hotly indignant over Caleb's posthumous cruelty. The woman had stood by him, after all. The woman had done nothing sinful. The woman had been a loyal and very patient wife.

"Was it because he found out about me, do you think, Mr. . . . ?"

"Marr. Joseph Marr."

"Mr. Marr? I mean, he found out there was . . . me, and he was angry?"

"How much do you know about your mother's history, Miss Keyne?"

"Oh, I know that she was married and that my father died and that she was terribly poor and had me, a little tiny girl, on her hands and this job was offered only to a woman without family ties. So, you see, she put me into a school under the care of a very wonderful . . . a darling"—Sally's voice paid its quivering tribute to Miss Mary—"school teacher. So there I stayed and had lots of friends and invitations and she sent me an allowance and gave me advantages. Piano and fencing and dancing and horseback riding."

Marr hissed, drawing in an anxious breath. He feared for the salvation represented by possible large savings. But Sally did not get the connection of ideas.

"And every now and then she'd come to see me. And she always wrote to me."

"U-hum. That's where she betrayed herself. Someone, I think it must have been one of the household, gossiped to Caleb about those letters and he sent an investigator. Yes, Miss Keyne, you were detected and what's more, Caleb discovered the name and history of your father. Mrs. Winter was married first to a John Keyne. He was a sailor and his death was reported in a South American rumpus somewhere. That was about a year after your birth."

"She married my father in the west, didn't she?"

"In San Francisco. Allow me to say only this. I think it would have been kinder to you, Miss Sally, if your mother had been more frank, not only with her employer, but with her child."

Sally gathered together quick excuses. "She was so

anxious to give me everything she could, to keep her position and . . ."

"Yes, yes. Well, what she has actually given you is . . ."

"But I've had Miss Mary Culpepper," cried Sally. "Indeed, I have," and she laughed shakily and then the crystal stood on her lashes and fell to her cheeks. "Of course you don't know Miss Mary and it must sound pretty funny but it means just everything to me." She rose. "I'd better go up to Mother now. I don't mind anything, if only she will get well."

She swept away her tears, walked over to the lawyer behind the desk and held out her wet hand. "Thank you, Mr. Marr. You've been kind. I think I can take it all right."

He shook her hand. "She looks out at a man the way a good boy should," thought Marr, and loved her.

"One thing . . . this nephew, Obadiah Crewe, do you know anything about him, Mr. Marr?"

"Only that his father was a bad lot and his mother quite unacceptable to the family; and never accepted."

"And when will he be coming to . . . to take over . . . everything?"

"I had a wire from him. He's on his way. He gave me no definite date. As yet, he doesn't know just what is waiting for him here."

Sally made a quaint and wry grimace. "It's an ill wind, isn't it, Mr. Marr? One of the things about getting older is that proverbs sort of begin to come true."

She went out, throwing back at him over her shoulder just before she started up the stairs a look that was not boyish at all: a lovely, laughing, sorrowful and frightened look. "Gad," thought the old man stamping about and gathering up his papers, "if I don't find myself hating that Obadiah. A Yankee sounding sort of name if ever I heard one!"

Chapter 5

There are two sympathetic pangs most difficult to bear: one, that of the old for the agonies of youth; the other, as keen, of the young for their beloved old. Beside her mother's bed all night—the enormous bed that Isabella had shared with her husband and must so often have lain awake in, her secret sweet and heavy on her heart!—Sally sat, the strong hand in both her own. She ached with her wish to take upon herself that helpless anguish.

Towards morning, she felt a motion of the hand, stood up and looked at Isabella's face. Its flush had gone so that it looked darkly pale, the eyes turned towards her and one-half of the mouth moved with difficulty.

"Poor baby! I meant it for the best." Tears ran in a narrow bright channel to the pillow.

"Mother darling! I don't care a bit. I'm absolutely, honestly *happy* to be with you, to take care of you. You do understand me, don't you, dear?"

"Yes."

"And you believe me. You must. Look ... I'm not crying. I'm perfectly cheerful, or would be, if you were well. I'm smiling, see? I don't care a pin for the big old house and everything. It isn't as if I'd had my childhood here. Listen, Mother sweet, just as soon as you are well enough, we'll go away. We'll have a little home together somewhere. Won't that be nicer, really? I think it will."

Mrs. Winter moved her head negatively.

"Can't do that. I've thought. I'll have to stay. I can arrange for you to go. I haven't a cent, Sally, to make a new home for us. I'll have to keep on here, work for Mr. Crewe."

This speech took an interminable while and infinite effort of the hampered mouth. It would have been obvious to Sally that her mother had suffered a partial paralysis, even if the doctor had not said, "She's not old and she's strong and active. She'll get back the use of that right side. It'll take time and patience and some expense. Electric treatments, exercises, massage."

"Don't you worry, Mother darling," she managed now to say cheerfully, putting down her head beside her mother's; "the doctor says you are going to get all right again. I'm going to stay with you and we'll work it out together. We'll be happy, too. It's not half bad to keep house, not if we have each other. Maybe Obadiah will be a sweet old gentleman. And, look here, Mother, I'm glad, though it sounds selfish, that you spent the money the way you did and didn't save it. Because I've had a wonderful life so far and not a bother in the world and I've been taught all sorts of things that will come in useful. And I've made friends. Besides, I'm braver because of what Miss Mary's taught me."

Mrs. Winter tried to turn her head and probe her daughter's look; she reached up with her well hand and touched the ruffled hair.

"Sweet! You *are* brave, aren't you? You look . . . like . . . Jackie."

And then she closed her eyes and went to sleep.

Sally dared to get into her wrapper and lie down on the sofa, well provided with little pillows and an old-fashioned afghan. This she pulled up over her body which was chill and shivering in reaction from the shock.

She lay there and thought about the future . . . and about Robin. He would come over to see her in the great Crewe House, and she would be keeping house for Mr. Obadiah Crewe. Because certainly her mother would have to use her as proxy until she was well. Sally would be a sort of upper servant, perhaps she'd have to wear a uniform. And Robin would see her as a cheap pretender, almost as an imposter. "I'm sure you ride to hounds . . ." Sally flopped over on her face and bit her pillow trying not to sob aloud. It had been terribly short, her ecstasy of homecoming. The world, she told herself with bitterness, is not going to be *my* oyster. This brought her back to Miss Mary's room filled with the quiet color of sunset and with serious girl faces all turned to Miss Mary's resolute, marching presence, head up, hands behind her back.

"I'd like you to remember that the first man to open an oyster was in search of food. The discovery of pearls must always remain a happy accident. Children, I want you to open your oysters with an eye to nourishment."

Sally found it necessary to choke down sudden, most unexpected laughter. Miss Mary was so funny and so cute. Well, after all, Sally Keyne's oyster was open for nourishment. She and her mother had a home, a job, a good monthly wage, more than a livelihood. They could save, now, for future liberty. There were a lot of people who'd shout for joy to change places with Isabella and her daughter. Men and women and children without any security at all, like that copper-faced fellow to whom she had refused a lift. It hadn't been a gracious gesture, nor a generous one. Perhaps it had lost him some prospective job. He'd been fired from the St. Charles garage, wanted to get somewhere else. Perhaps she had forced him to go hungry, shelterless. She could not seem to remember now why she had felt it to be so imperative that he be thrown down from his cheerful perch on the front seat beside George into the road. Because he'd been pushed against her on the hotel steps and Robin had quite unjustly knocked him down? Because he was shabby and rough and ugly and had hard blue eyes and a blunt, outspoken tongue? Not very sufficient reasons.

She slept and offered the tramp a ride in the back seat with Miss Keyne and said—a very generous and democratic dreamer!—"And you may call me Sally, if you like, Vincent"—awake she would not perhaps have remembered his name—"but I can't let you kiss me because I didn't even let Robin do that."

There was no need to engage a nurse for Mrs. Winter. Her colored maid, Zona, would have run a professional attendant out of the room. "If anyone's goin' to handle my Mis' Winter, that's me," said Zona, tall, strong and largely smiling. Early too was neat and handy. The doctor said that for the present there was no treatment but one of perfect quiet. "Avoid any excitement."

Sally told her mother, "I've taken complete charge of everything. I've thought it all out and I know what to do. I want you, for my sake, Mother, just to forget all about everything except only getting well."

But Mrs. Winter muttered with that painful effort, "I've got to move out of this room, Sally. That must be done before Mr. Crewe arrives."

"All right," said Sally rather shortly, "I'll attend to that, if the doctor thinks it safe."

"My old room," said Mrs. Winter, "is at the far end of this wing." She spoke as though she had a yearning to be in it. "It's a lovely room. And there's a nice small sort of dressing room next door that you can have, Sally. And a wee sitting room. And a bath just opposite for both of us. We'll be very comfortable."

Her eyes and crippled speech, however, as soon as she included Sally in the move, had become anxious.

"Of course we will. I like that end of the house. You can see the river. And I'm going to take possession of your workroom, Mother. And get things all lined up. If I make mistakes, you can straighten them out afterwards. Now, not one other word or *think*, do you hear me? That horrible Obadiah nephew won't be moving in for ages probably." Mrs. Winter was actually moved to a sound like laughter by Sally's tone and the lively contortion of her face. "We have plenty of time to get used to being double housekeeper."

She went down to the "work-and-ordering" room, shut herself in and leaned against the door. "This room," she thought, not foreseeing fortunately all that it might enclose for her, "is going to see a lot of me." She let its sober walls, closely shadowed windows and sombre leather furniture absorb her so that she became one of its possessions. She began then to walk about, smoking a cigarette. After her third, she sat down before the big table desk and took out the account books and the recipe books and the memorandum books.

Mrs. Winter had kept clear and accurate notes on everything.

Sally found a list of house and outdoor servants like a Dramatis Personæ. It was dated only April of this year so that she thought it would serve her present necessity.

"Indoor servants (colored):

Trot Selby, *cook.*

Emily, *assistant.*

Maybelle and Lottie May, *kitchen maids.*

Charles Brown, *butler.*

Henry, Charles' nephew, *house man.*

Oliver, Charles' cousin, *second man.*

Little Walter and Luncheon, Charles' great nephews: *errands, fires, boots and shoes, etc. N. B. Remind C. again not to spank them in the pantry.*

Zona Graham, *my personal maid, fine washing, mending, etc.*

Grace, *parlor maid.*

Fair, *chambermaid.*

Lightning, *chamber maid. (Doubtful. Vain and lazy, nice to look at.)*

Benjamina Jones, *laundress.*

Jimmie, her husband, *waits on her.*

Sweet and Ruby, *assistant laundresses.*

And, in very fine writing, "Monkey ... *no use. C. W. prejudiced,*" with no further explanatory or descriptive comment.

Garage and Garden and Stables (white):

George Elmer, chauffeur. (Sally flushed.)

Tony Preston, *second chauffeur and mechanic.*

Ernest Brunn, *gardener. (His wife Anna, and Nan, daughter, help with outfit. Ernest permitted hire extra colored help busy seasons.)*

John and Michael, *gardener assistants.*

Godfrey Nunn, *in charge of stables.*

Jock Nunn, *stable man.*

Fenwick.

Sterne. *(C. W. won't cut down on stables. Great nuisance and expense.)*

Opposite each name was jotted down the wages paid per month.

Sally sat back in her chair and ran her fingers through her mane. Her heart was bumping at her ribs. She sleeked down the shining crest, tightened her mouth and, looking very pale, pressed her finger hard on the button of her desk bell. Then she sat up straight and waited.

Henry appeared.

"Henry, I want you to tell all the indoor servants, expect Zona and Early who are with Mrs. Winter, to come here right away so that I can explain something to them."

Henry gravely bowed and disappeared. He had the aspect of an apparition, a sort of black skull countenance and long dangling hands, a full three wrist lengths, Sally thought, below his cuffs. The whites of his eyes were yellow. "He must have malaria or hookworm," Sally decided and wondered if her mother had a book of Household Remedies and a medicine chest somewhere.

Gradually the room filled with solemn and respectful people. Even the two tiny boys, Walter and Luncheon, who must on no account be spanked in the pantry, came, fidgeting with their feet and fingers. They were dressed alike in white shirts and neat little black overalls. They wore sneakers and made no sound whatever when they walked.

When all were present or accounted for . . . "Jim was just sent down to do my errands," enormous Benjamina explained in a gusty whisper staring at Sally as though she had never seen a blonde girl of nineteen before. Lightning could not be located. "She's a no-account hysterious gal," Charles said severely and marshalled Luncheon and Walter to a corner where they were told to "Keep theirselves entirely unsuggested."

Sally looked at them all and smiled. A flashing as of white banners immediately returned her salute. Then gravely and slowly she made her speech.

"Since I came here yesterday," she said, "everything

has changed for my mother and for me. Mr. Caleb Winter, who had a perfect right, of course, to do with his belongings what he thought fit, made a surprising will. He did not leave anything at all to my mother."

A sigh as of sympathy, amazement, grief went round.

"He left this house and place and all his money to a nephew of his first wife. His name is Mr. Obadiah Crewe and he will be coming here soon to take possession."

Benjamina began to rock. "O de whole worl' surely come to end," and for an instant it looked to Sally as though there might be an outbreak of hysteria. But Charles took Benjamina by her immense arm, shook her and told her not to "exhibitionate herself."

"My mother is not going to leave you!" Sally cried quickly. "She is sick now but she will be getting well soon and meantime I am going to try to keep house. Mr. Winter," Sally hated the uncontrollable warmth of her face, "wanted my mother to stay on here in her old capacity of housekeeper and to take care of this beautiful house for a while in any case ... under its new master. So I'm going to ask you to stand by me and help me all you possibly can. You know my mother's ways and you can come to me about everything. I want to spare her any bother so I hope you won't bother *me* much."

Charles, with his soft round eyes, seemed to gather up the sentiment of his fellows. "We all is mighty appreciative for your open-speakingness, Miss Sally," he said, "and we all aim to stand right by you through your trials and help you out of the deep waters to a firm footin' on the further shores. Old capacity or young capacity we ain't any of us carin' just so's we make that passage smooth."

There was a brief outbreak of applause after which Sally with thanks and reassuring speeches let them go. She retained Charles for an instant. "Charles, do you know anyone that works here that could possibly be known as *Monkey?*"

"Yes'm. That's Mr. Winter's personal man, Miss Sally. He's gone away for a vacation pendin' further orders."

"How does he spell his name?"

Charles laughed sweetly. "How do I know? Call him Mr. Monkey. He's a West Indian gent'man."

The white people took her tidings in a very different fashion and spirit from the blacks. The head gardener, Brunn, a small, sun-soaked Swiss, brooded a minute sifting imaginary earth between his thumb and fingers and then, smiling his face into a hundred wrinkles, asked her if she'd care to see "his beds." Sally for an hour forgot her anxieties. This man was so entirely absorbed in seed and soil and plant and produce that he carried her completely out of her own world into his. It did not seem to occur to Ernest Brunn that his livelihood might be threatened by the arrival of a new owner. It was "my asparagus, my tomatoes and my cucumber frames."

In the stables Sally came upon a problem of unforeseen bitterness. Jock, the son of Godfrey Nunn, a goodlooking, eager English lad, whose father had listened with no comment whatever beyond a quick and sympathetic glance to her story of the will, took her about to see the horses.

"I've been gentling a pretty saddle mare for your use, miss. We've called her Star," said Jock.

Sally stood still. She turned upon the young man so pale a face that he drew in his breath audibly.

"Oh, I can't bear it. I can't bear to see her, Jock. You don't know how I feel about horses. Is she beautiful?"

"I'm afraid she is, miss. But," cried Jock, his blue eyes glittering, "if the man's a single gentleman, he'll be glad to have help exercising the animals. Mr. Winter, he just kept up the stables out of respect for his wife's memory; I mean his first wife's, miss. The Crewes were always great riders, miss. And, anyway, Miss Keyne, it's none of my business, of course, but this mare was meant for you and your mother got it before she knew a word about this will."

Sally looked at him then with all her eyes and rubbed her hair about on her forehead. "I'm just all mixed up, Jock. To tell you the truth, I don't know where I stand at all. But, if you'll forgive me, I don't think I can bear to see that Star today. Not just today."

Jock said mournfully, "And I can quite understand your feeling, miss."

His eyes held battle light. Sally knew, with a glow of comfort and reassurance, that he wore her colors.

When she went down to the garage, after her sad and lonely lunch, George greeted her, half in embarrassment and half in sympathy. "Mrs. Winter just bought you a nice little roadster for your special use," said George, after he had heard and digested her news. "I don't just know what the situation is, but it's certainly your own car, bought and paid for before"—as George insisted upon calling it—"the crash."

Again Sally rubbed her bang. "Honestly, George, I don't know what to think."

"Well, Miss Keyne, if I was you I'd just sort of take possession of whatever you can lay your two hands on before ever this chap, this Mr. Crewe, gets his own hands on everything. How about trying your machine out now? Just a spin. It's a fine day and you're looking peaked, and no wonder."

Sally, as though compelled, got into the car and laid her "two hands" upon its shining wheel. Three minutes later she was flying up a polished highway against the flowing pressure of high speed.

Chapter 6

It was a noble countryside, rich, green, white-fenced and wooded; for the most part privately and largely owned. The hamlets were prosperous and nicely cared for, the highways beautifully bordered and well kept. From her first hilltop, Sally looked down on the local country club with its fairways and little red flags. She could see the golfers moving in their tranced fashion after the white, caddy-tended balls. "That's where I'd be soon if I were really the daughter of Crewe House," and she remembered the house parties she had planned, the visitors. She would have returned her friends' generous hospitalities in full measure, running over. It was only her eyes now that ran over so that she was forced to stop and blow her nose. But again she pumped up courage and refurbished her philosophy. Anyway, there's no use crying about it. I've got to get used to the idea. After all, I only thought myself rich and important for about forty-eight hours. It certainly had not become a habit. There's nothing shameful in my father's having been a sailor and my mother a housekeeper.

But, better than any of this self-administered wisdom, speed served to comfort her. She had the feeling of outdistancing distress. She was annoyed, therefore, by the necessity for a detour which, however, eventually so pleased her with its vagaries and wooded banks that she was furious when a big car screamed at her insolently, shot past and leaving her scant space above a ditch, enveloped her in a choking cloud of dust. Angry, she stepped on her gas, sat straight and gripped her wheel. On the first straight bit, she had the satisfaction of passing a driver who had become complacent over his triumphant lead and of flinging back upon him in her turn a suffocating mantle. Now, the race was on. One half mile further, and she was again outdistanced but, this time, on the hill ahead the larger car slowed down, an arm emerged with narrow signalling hand. The driver stopped, dismounted and, to her alarm, stood straight in her way with his arms spread out.

An instant of heart-pounding later, she recognized him and jumped up behind her wheel, jamming on the brakes.

"Robin Ashe!"

He was already on her running board.

"I recognized you as you went past me, Sally. Am I a lucky man? Here I was on my way back from trying to see you. I've only this one afternoon. Got to get back to college tomorrow. So I took a chance following you down from Baltimore; pretended I had to see my family. I nearly died when they told me at your house that you'd just gone out."

She saw in his dark eyes, fitted slantwise into his narrow charming head, that he had been thinking of her as constantly as she, for all the stress of recent circumstance, had been of him.

"I'm pretty keen about myself for recognizing you," he said. "Most girls look so different in broad daylight in the skirt and sweater uniform you all wear but you, you just look prettier, Sally. You'd be surprised how dizzy-glad I am to see you again."

"I wouldn't be surprised. I'm sort of gauging you by . . . me. We did have fun in Baltimore!"

"We did. But what's happened to you since, Sally? You . . . your eyes have changed."

"My mother was taken very ill. Suddenly."

"What a tough break. I am sorry . . . awfully."

"I tell you what, Robin. Come back to the house with me now. It's not far. I can give you tea or something. I'd like you to see the place before . . . I mean . . ." Her cheeks glowed. "I want to tell you all the queer things that have been happening to me since . . ." She stopped absolutely aghast. "Was that only two days before yesterday, Robin?"

"About three years and a half ago. Three and a half long and misspent years. All right. I'll follow you. Let's go. I don't want to waste any more of my youth. Make the home run snappy, will you, Sally? I shan't mind your dust, knowing it's yours. Oh, darling, darling dust!" laughed Robin so that she laughed with him.

Yes, she would take him back and give him tea, pretending, for just one hour, that she was the true daughter of Crewe House. But, before he left, she'd tell him what she really was. He must, on no account, nor by any stupid accident, hear the truth from any other tongue but hers. Of course, he isn't an old-fashioned Victorian snob. He won't care so much, even if he is born a Virginian with that "inherited look" . . . but she could not help remembering uncomfortably that slight change in the expression of his eyes and voice when he had said, "*The* Crewe Mansion?" There had been snobs at St. Sylvester's.

And now, she couldn't ever ride with him to hounds!

First Sally hung her head and then she threw it up and back with that toss of her blonde panache which had reassured Marr as to her ability to "take it." "If he's worth his salt, he won't care. If he likes me honestly, he'll only feel sorry and anxious to help. If he isn't like that . . . why then," said Sally to herself, "to hell with him!" Miss Mary might have been shocked but then again Miss Mary might not have been. Startled . . . she'd open her eyes.

As always, the visualization of Miss Mary steadied Sally. She looked altogether calm and cool and level-eyed by the time she welcomed her friend into the house of Crewe.

Just inside the door Charles met her.

"Oh, Miss Sally," said Charles in a low voice of discretion, "*the* Mr. Crewe has just arrived. He's in the big drawing room with Mr. Marr. I was to tell you to join them as soon as you came in."

Sally turned back to face Robin, who was still outside the door.

"Robin, I'm dreadfully sorry. I can't tell you how terribly I feel after making you drive all this way back. But it's just not possible for me, after all, to ask you in for tea. Something has happened. There's someone I must see." Her distress dilated her pupils so that her great eyes looked black.

Robin captured her hand. His own eyes were filled with her trouble and had forgotten any disappointment of their own.

"Sally dear, I'm sorry. You're shaking, aren't you? Something pretty rotten's happening to you. Can't I help?"

"You do help . . . caring a little . . ."

"Caring," he said earnestly, "a lot. Will you write and tell me? May I write and tell *you?*"

"Yes, Robin. But let me write first. I've got to go in. Thank you. Do please forgive me. Thank you," she turned from him and whispered, *"dear."*

He went down two steps, ran up them and, this time asking for no permission, kissed her.

Sally watched him go. When the sound of his car was no longer audible she turned and went again into the house.

"Charles, please tell someone to take my . . . the roadster back to the garage. Charles, did you say . . . in the big drawing room?"

"Yes, miss."

She waited. Charles went softly away. His steps expressed his sympathy for her.

"I'd rather die," Sally thought, speaking really only just beneath her breath, "than go in there and see that man. But there are things in life that just have to be *done.*"

She walked across the hall. "I wish I didn't look so sort of warm and dusty." She set her hand on a knob and turned and opened.

Down the great length of the room she saw little Joseph Marr, looking like a figurine. His companion stood with his back turned staring out of a window so bright with afternoon sun that he was perfectly invisible . . . only the rather heavy outline of a man.

She came slowly forward. It was such a beautiful room! Only yesterday she had so loved it!

"Ah, Miss Keyne, here you are." Marr came trotting forward. "That's very nice . . . quite timely. Er . . . er . . . Mr. Crewe, if you please, this . . . er . . . is the young lady."

Mr. Crewe heavily and sombrely and without speech

turned himself about. He was shabby and there was dust on his shoes.

"But this isn't possible," Sally heard herself saying not loudly at all. "There's some mistake. This can't be Obadiah Crewe, Mr. Marr. I know this man. His name is . . . Vincent."

Chapter 7

"Obadiah Vincent Crewe," the young tramp answered for himself. "You wouldn't expect me to call myself Obadiah, would you?"

Mr. Marr cackled uneasily. "Well, well, so you have a previous acquaintanceship. That should help to oil the machinery. Now, Mr. Crewe, I'll leave you. I have some business to attend to. I think we've gone over the essentials. If I may wait on you tomorrow . . . ?"

"You mean come up here? Don't put yourself out, sir. I'll run down to your office first thing tomorrow morning. Thanks."

He spoke bluntly but his voice was neither coarse nor rough.

"I think I may leave you in Miss Sally's hands. She can, I'm sure, make you feel at home."

Marr then went out, pretending not to see the wild entreaty in poor Sally's eyes.

When not only the drawing room door but the house door had been audibly shut, Vincent came closer, his hands thrust down deep into the pockets of his overalls, his under lip pushed out. "So you're the housekeeper's daughter, are you?" he said. "I might have figured that out for myself. The folks that take up the most space are pretty generally the little folks. All right, Miss Sally, how about getting me a drink of something and a ham sandwich? I've got a hunger and a thirst. This darn mortuary establishment has got a cellar or a sideboard, I figure."

"I'll send Charles to you with a tray." Sally's own lips were dry. She started up the room.

"Hold on. Come back with the stuff yourself, can't you? I don't want to eat alone in this funeral parlor

54

surrounded," he gave an ugly look to the portraits, "by mourning relatives. Besides, I've got a lot of things to ask you.

"Judas," he exclaimed, as she did not answer, "you walk like a duchess with a grouch. What's the matter? Don't you like me being in my own house?"

Sally turned. If being like a duchess with a grouch meant making the most of her inches and having eyes, enormous and glittering in a perfectly colorless face, she certainly deserved the epithet.

"Until this morning," she said, her voice travelling high and clear as though on a silver wire beyond his reach, "until this morning, Mr. Crewe, I thought this was *my* house, my home, as it has been my mother's for twelve years. I can see that you haven't had the training of a gentleman but you should have at least half the nature of one and I think you owe to my mother and me a certain degree of consideration, of ordinary courtesy. We are in a terrible and humiliating situation here. We can't even leave yet because my mother is very ill and she is without a penny in the world. A few days ago she was the mistress of this place. Her husband, who was your uncle by marriage, died not seven days ago. I am going to ask you, if you please, to give our situation some thought. You may not be a kind man ... no doubt you've had a hard time ..."

"I am remembering," he interrupted, "the consideration you handed out to me when I was having a hard time, about forty-eight hours ago in Baltimore. I didn't know then that I was anybody's heir. I guess I was in a humiliating situation myself a couple of times back there. Once, when I was begging a lift of your chauffeur and getting thrown out on my ear, and another once, when you got your young man to punch me in the mouth and then pulled away your skirts and went off, leaving me to get kicked about by a bunch of hotel frogs. Well, you may be a kind young gentlewoman in every sense of the word, but I can't say I've seen any unmistakable evidence of it so far."

He was standing very close now, facing her down. Sally had never met before eyes so cold, so bitter, so hateful of herself. "Now, look here. I'm sorry for your mother. But, as far as you and me are concerned, this is the way of it. You had the whip hand and I'll say you used it. Now, I've got it and I'm going to use it. I've been taught how, plenty." He stopped and Sally saw that he was breathing fast. "Go on now, will you? And get me that whiskey I asked for. I tell you I've got a *thirst*."

Sally ran out and, using both her hands, the one to steady the other, quietly and closely shut the door. Panting and shaking, she stood for a minute in the hall, then went onto the front porch. She had a wild improbable hope that Robin would be back. He would take her away to his own safe home, to the mother from whom he had inherited his mouth and smile. But the vistaed driveway was empty, its shadow lying undisturbed in regular bars. She remembered that she must give an order for this employer of hers who had, it would seem, emphatically "a thirst." She hurried in and pressed the bell on her desk in the workroom.

"Charles, will you take Mr. Crewe some ham and chicken sandwiches and whiskey?"

"Into the drawing room, Miss Sally?"

"He said so."

"Plain water or charged, miss?"

Sally laughed breathlessly. "I don't know. Perhaps you'd better ask him."

"Shall I get you a little something yourself, Miss Sally, ma'am? You're looking a mite pale."

"No, Charles. But will you please have dinner sent upstairs to me? I think I'll eat it in my mother's room this evening."

"Yes, miss. She's had herself moved, Miss Sally, ma'am, whilst you was out in yo' li'l car, and stood it very well."

"Moved? Oh, is she really all right? In that room then, Charles. I'll be going up to her and I'll stay with her now the rest of the afternoon and evening. I won't be coming down."

Charles hesitated an instant at the threshold and rolled back his spaniel eyes. He lowered his beautiful soft voice. "What sort of gen'man is he, Miss Sally?"

"Charles, don't ask me. I can't tell you what sort of gentleman he is."

"A . . . a regular Crewe, miss?"

"What would a regular Crewe be like?"

"A very sweet gen'man, Miss Sally."

"I don't think he's at all a regular Crewe, Charles. But go on in with the sandwiches and whiskey and you will certainly see for yourself what sort of sweet gentleman we've got." A sense of the ridiculous here came running back into her consciousness like a deserter in haste to make amends and she found herself laughing like a girl well-interested and well-amused.

The accession of interest and of amusement carried her successfully through the difficult necessity of announcing to her mother that the heir had arrived. She was able, under the influence of humor, to give to her description of him a light and cheerful color. Afterwards, however, safe in her own small room so different from the one that had been happily made ready for her, the child's courage first faltered and then collapsed. She sat, stiff and pale, completely recaptured by a discomfort which amounted, as darkness fell, to fear. A strange man was in control of her life and this strange man hated her.

In her nineteen years, Sally had had a far greater experience of courtesy than of rudeness, of friendliness than of anger, of love than of hate. But she could not disguise from herself now, remembering the tone of Vincent's voice and the look in his slate eyes, that she had now excited hatred in a dangerous quarter. It is hard for anyone, especially for the young and even more especially for the young girl, to endure patiently a completely false image of herself in another person's mind. Sally, writhing vainly, saw herself as she must exist in the mind of Vincent Crewe: a snobbish and vulgar young woman, a sort of over-educated servant, who, uncertain of her own social standing, was quick to belittle that of others, cruel to what she fancied an inferior, apt to put such a fellow with emphasis into his place. She could not help hating the holder of this image; the more so because it had been evoked by her own unthinking behavior.

She hated Vincent chiefly because she had induced him to hate her, but also because he, a rough and ignorant man, was in a sense now her superior, the master of her fate. There lay her mother, helpless, in need of treatments that must be expensive and prolonged, dependent for shelter, food, her hope of life itself, upon the brutal terms of Caleb's will. "I hereby bequeath the shelter of my roof and wages ... to be enjoyed on condition that she faithfully and humbly remain obedient to the orders of Obadiah Crewe ..." And, under the circumstances, this condition must be fulfilled by Sally Keyne, who was by no means of a humble spirit. Faithful she would be, loyal to her mother, but humble she was not. At this moment, defiance was the breath of her nostrils, a defiance only just able to keep abreast of fear.

For what did she or anyone else know about this man? His credentials, she supposed, must have been in order, he must have been able to satisfy legal requirements as to his identity, but of his history, his past conduct, his record as a citizen, which of them all knew anything? And here was she, a girl of nineteen, left to his mercy, a sort of peon in the vast, complicated house; her protectors an ancient colored man with his cohorts, and a paralyzed invalid who must on no account be troubled, excited or disturbed.

The night, when she came to this final gloomy period, was creeping up like a floodtide to Crewe House; its chimney alone held a faint last look of day and, as though to increase her sense of eerie helplessness, a wind was rising and black clouds turned themselves like immense wheels out of the east. From her window she could see these purple cylinders crush out a few faint and early stars. The trees turned too and made a noise of disaster and alarm.

Chapter 8

That sad high wind had perhaps a fearful sound to another person in Crewe House, for the nephew of Jessica, in this first night in his new home, found it difficult to sleep. He forsook the high four poster in which Caleb Winter had died and which had been reluctantly turned down for him by the scared chambermaids, and lay upon the sofa, his arms crossed back of his head against a mound of little pillows. The silent and complicated mansion of his life with all its rooms and passages lay in his memory with a greater sense of reality than those of his material shelter and he could not hinder a perpetual wandering, a haunting of its darkest corners by his own tormented mind.

So it was that Obadiah Vincent Crewe rose early, grateful for day, and went out into a still morning to examine his estate.

He visited the stables, the garden and the garage, renewing an acquaintance with the chauffeur, George Elmer, who wore during this encounter a somewhat sheepish air. Having eaten a hearty breakfast with Ernest Brunn, his wife and pretty daughter, who were sitting down to theirs at the instant of their new employer's appearance, he set out on foot for the village of Hanbury, two or three miles from his front gate. In Hanbury's dry goods store he bought himself a complete new outfit of clothing, shed the overalls and khaki shirt and then looked up his lawyer, Joseph Marr.

Marr had a small neat office above a stationer's shop and here Crewe found him, although the hour was earlier than usual for the beginning of the legal business. Marr had no mind to miss his client's promised visit.

"Good morning, good morning, Mr. Crewe. I hope

you rested comfortably in your new home. You have been well advised already, I perceive."

Crewe looked bewildered until Marr pushed to him across the desk a copy of the morning news. There he could read for himself the story of Caleb's will with its studied insult to his unfortunate widow and a highly colored description of his own sudden elevation from the estate of tramp to that of millionaire. Of Sally Keyne there was no mention. The fact of Mrs. Winter's earlier and secret marriage had evidently not leaked out.

The hero of this tale sat down to read it, bending forward with his elbows planted on far apart knees. Marr thought that never had he seen a young man in such fortunate circumstances at so great a disadvantage, so surly or so obviously depressed. His face turned a deep copper color while he read and presently he rumpled up poor Marr's nicely folded sheet and threw it down on the floor. He took out a can of cheap tobacco, rolled and lighted himself a cigarette.

"Hell! I'll be on every sucker list in the country. They'll be trying to kidnap me next. How the heck do those news devils get on a man's scent so quick?"

He smoked and brooded, his head in his hand, elbows still set upon his knees, Marr watching him. The fellow's body, Marr thought, was handsomer than his head which was too small for its big throat and shoulders and had a predatory outline, hawk's or Roman legionary's. The apparent heaviness of physique was caused by the muscular development of physical labor, which always makes a man look bulky in civilized dress. Crewe should be advised to wear loose tweeds, he should dress carefully and very well. "Heaven knows," thought Caleb's lawyer, "he can afford it." He must be told to let his hair grow and to get a gentleman's cut. That horrible army shave has left a paper white band across the back of his head, above his ears and at the top of his forehead. At this point, the subject of Marr's sartorial and tonsorial observations stood up.

"Look here, Marr, being a millionaire goes down good with me but how can I lay hands on some cash pronto? I haven't got a copper. Had to borrow from a guy to get down here. I guess you noticed the reversed charge on my answer to your wire."

"I can easily fix that for you." Marr too rose. "Suppose I take you around to the bank. I can arrange an advance, you can make a deposit and open a check account. That ought to simplify things for you. By the way what name will you be using? The will and the newspapers have you Obadiah."

Crewe went into a long fit of brooding.

"I reckon I'll leave it at that," he said sullenly. "It's not a pretty name but it's got one advantage, nobody that ever knew me before will think it's mine. I won't be getting every bum I ever owed a buck to, down on my neck."

He stood with his arms hanging rather far out at his sides, his fingers curled in. Marr wondered if he'd had some experience in the ring. He stood so balanced on the balls of his feet ready for a spring. He had that sort of eye too, watchful for the shape of a blow in the eye that it encountered. Watching him, Marr had suddenly a contrasting vision: he saw a tawny-haired child with an enormous pair of shining and open eyes. This fellow was not just exactly the man Marr would have chosen to set as guardian over the helpless life of a girl like Sally Keyne. She had her mother, of course, and a raft of tired and respectable servants but, still . . .

"How did you and Miss Sally get on together?" he asked as they went down the street.

"Pretty good considering," was Crewe's casual reply. "She can't be feeling very kind towards me under the circumstances."

"But you had met before."

"Can't say we met; we had a sort of contact. In fact, she had me thrown out of the front seat of her limousine. I begged a lift off that guy, Elmer. I was trying to get down here, just like she was. Sort of funny when you come to think of it."

"It is," Marr agreed drily and shooting a sidelong glance up at his companion, "it is, to say the least, very odd indeed, the whole concatenation of events."

Obadiah's lips moved silently. Marr thought that he was swearing under his breath but he was repeating the syllables of Marr's long word, "con . . . ca . . . ten . . . a

... tion." Having amused or annoyed himself thus for a moment he said aloud and with abruptness, "Do you think those two women, Mrs. Winter and her girl, will be bringing suit to break the will?"

Marr stopped, then trotted on. "Hardly. Hardly. The law in this part of the world is not particularly favorable and the fact of her long deception as to a previous marriage and the child kept on Caleb's money at a smart school would rather militate against her in a court. Besides, she would stand to lose a substantial sure income; three thousand six hundred a year is not to be sniffed at, Mr. Crewe."

"Who's sniffin'?"

"... with a free home and living expenses for both her daughter and herself. That is, of course, unless you object to the presence of this child ..."

"I could throw her out, eh, could I?"

Marr, very red in his cheekbones, said unwillingly, "I suppose you could but, er, naturally it would appear to me as ... to say the least ... an ungenerous gesture."

Obadiah laughed shortly, a sound not very reassuring to the anxious listener. It is always difficult for a lawyer to dislike a wealthy client but Marr found himself driven against his will further and further towards that most improvident emotion. He did not like this heavyset expressionless young tramp, mistrusted, even feared him. What had Caleb known of the life and training of the nephew he had so arbitrarily chosen to be his heir? This hard-eyed, close-cropped, heavy-jawed fellow might well have seen the inside of a prison. He was an ill-conditioned owner for beautiful Crewe House. Poor little lady Jessica! thought Joseph Marr, who had loved Caleb's first girl wife and had known something of her pathetic history, which had included and been overwhelmed by a tragically thwarted love.

In the interval between his visit to the bank and his return to his new home, Crewe entered the liquor store, the billiard parlor and the room behind the parlor. By the time he returned to the long stately drive flanked by its mighty trees, he was red-faced and inclined to step high over the bars of shade. A cur followed him up from the village.

For most of the afternoon he slept, stretched out on

a sofa of pale blue brocade, the cur thumping his tail against a Persian rug. He woke at five, sat up with a great scared start and found himself staring at the portrait of his aunt above a carven chimney piece. He was in the library of Crewe House and on either side of the chimney the walls were lined from floor to ceiling with shelves of books. A bow window at ground level opened on the ordered tulips which seemed to be dancing their way across the sills. Jessica Crewe, in the portrait, had an open-eyed slender face beneath the full pompadour and above the square-necked and puff-sleeved frock of a Gibson girl. She looked a trifle moqueuse with her small ears exposed, a tip-tilted nose and tucked-in-and-down-mouth corners. At this presentment of an aunt he had never known, Obadiah Vincent stared for a long while, rolling and smoking a series of cigarettes.

It would have been quite impossible for an observer to read his reflections, his eyes and mouth being the least betraying possible of human features. They seemed to be useful only as tools of sight and speech. They were, in fact, the features of a man whose emotional reactions have been, since babyhood, of not the slightest interest to anyone, not even to himself. For lack of audience and practice, they had almost lost their natural eloquence.

From the prolonged contemplation of Jessica Crewe, during which his own face began to acquire a faint reflection of that mocking and secretive look, the young man removed his eyes to the high shelves. Presently as though pulled up against his will he rose and, still smoking, walked along the walls, studying titles and muttering to himself. "Poetry," he said aloud without reflection, merely stating a discovery and took down into his big rough hands a tiny volume of tooled leather with gilt-edged delicate sheets. With this he returned to his love-seat, the cur anxiously returning with him.

Charles came in to turn on the lights.

"You'll hurt your eyes, sir."

At the soft, fatherly admonition, Crewe looked up, surprised.

"I reckon you're right." He laid the book down beside him on its face. Charles was now eyeing the cur with obvious disapprobation.

"How you like my dog?" asked Vincent.

"Well, sir, it ain't hardly for me to say, Mr. Crewe, but he don't look to me like a gen'man's dog, sir."

"He isn't. He belongs to me. You can look out for him, can't you? He should have a bath and be liberally defleaed. Also he needs a lining to his belly. His name," said Vincent, gravely, "is just . . . Dawg. Hi, Dawg, how you making? See, he knows his name already."

"Yes, sir," Charles smiled, "he sure do. I reckon he's a right smart animal. Hi, you Dawg, come along with me and git your dinner."

Before leaving with his low-class companion, however, Charles said, "Mr. Crewe, sir, Mr. Monkey's done come back and would powerful like if you could see him."

"Mr. . . . . Monkey?"

"Yes, sir. He was Mr. Winter's personal man, a Jamaican gentleman, sir. He's been in service a mighty long while here, Mr. Crewe. He worked for Miss Jessica's father, old Mr. Vincent Crewe, sir. He was valet for Miss Jessica's brother, too. Your pa, sir."

"Personal man! Look here, you all don't expect me to use a valet, do you?"

"Why yes, sir, we do. You'll surely need a man for your clothes and such, sir. Pressing and cleaning and keeping in order."

Vincent looked down at his solitary suit.

"Oh, will I? I kind of thought my housekeeper'd sew on my buttons and darn my socks."

"Oh no, sir! Hardly. Not Mrs. Winter nor Miss Keyne, Mister Obadiah. You wouldn't hardly expect that. Benjamina and Ruby do the general mending. Or Zona."

"O.K. Tell this Mr. Monkey to come along in. Wait a sec though, Charles."

Charles paused; the cur slinking beside him paused too and lifted his eyes from a hanging head anxiously. In his face too there was that expectation of the shadow of a blow, but his fashion of preparing for it was not as aggressive as his new master's.

To Charles' horror, Vincent then tore out a flyleaf

from the exquisite small volume he had laid aside and wrote carefully with a pencil stub from his vest pocket, a few lines.

"See that Miss Keyne gets this, will you, Charles?"

"Yes, sir."

Charles took the folded paper. "Do you want I should send Mr. Monkey to you upstairs whilst you dress, sir?"

"Dress? I'm all the dressed I'm going to be. Tell him to come in here now and make it snappy. I kind of thought I'd duck down to the river for a swim before supper. When do I get my supper, Charles?"

"At eight o'clock, sir."

"Eight? Well, that gives me plenty of time to wash back of the ears."

A few minutes later a small, thin old man in a neat, black, well-cut suit, came into the room, stopped just inside the threshold and bowed.

"Mr. Crewe: Sebastian Manchi, if you please, sir."

Vincent, who now stood staring out at the tulips and the evening meadows that held his swimming water, turned slowly about. There was always that heavy, almost lurching movement of his shoulders when he turned.

"By Judas," he said in his softest voice, "you're not British, are you?"

"Yes, sir," said the pale, ageless creature, "I am a British subject. I was born in Jamaica, sir."

"West Indian black, eh?"

The man's narrow, pale face contracted, as did his full lidded eyes, but he moved his mouth, which was thin and collapsed, into an inexpressive smile.

"I have a very small amount of African blood on my maternal grandfather's side, sir."

"How you spell your name?"

"M-A-N-C-H-I."

"Sounds Spanish."

"I dare say it is, Mr. Crewe. Shall I lay out your dinner clothes, sir?"

"You expect me to keep you on, eh?"

The man's face acquired a look so curiously sharp and sheathed, that Vincent's attention remained fixed.

"Why yes, sir," he said. "I hardly think you could do

without me, sir. And, if I may say so, Mr. Winter by the terms of his will made me a sort of fixture, if I may say so."

"You may say so. I remember, now, you were mentioned in the will amongst some other servants. To my man Sebastian Manchi, 2500 dollars per year during his lifetime on condition ... my uncle-in-law was a great hand for conditions. Well, I guess I'm saddled with you for a while. I'll probably outlive you, if I may say so, Manchi. *Probably*. Now, listen to me. This is the one and only outfit I possess. What will you do about that?"

Manchi drew in a sharp, shocked breath.

"You will be going to New York, sir, of course, for the—er—the replenishment of your wardrobe."

"I will not!"

"If I may say so, sir, I should then advise that you let me take very careful tailor's measurements, sir, and make out a comprehensive list of your needs and then allow me to go north to Mr. Winter's tailor, if you can spare me, sir. He was an old gentleman of course and didn't need the wardrobe you will require, sir. Golf, riding, cocktails, dinners, formal and informal, balls ..."

Vincent stood in his pose of a boxer and stared.

"And, if I may say so, sir, I wouldn't go about socially, sir," Manchi put his narrow pale head aside, "until your hair has grown out a little. I really wish, sir, that you had waited for a bit of advice from me, sir, before you had your recent haircut."

After one of his long staring silences, Vincent pulled himself together with a jerk.

"You knew my parents?"

Manchi bowed.

"My father? My mother?"

"Yes, sir, if I may say so, rather intimately."

" 'Intimately' I reckon is your middle name. What'd you think of them?"

"It would hardly be my place to express an opinion, sir."

Vincent gave out his sudden yell of laughter, a sound at once demoniac and boyish, sometimes exchangeable adjectives.

"Good alibi." He was abruptly gloomy. "Did you

know my father ran off and left my mother and me in South America? He died raving mad with liquor in San Francisco."

Manchi bowed. "Yes, sir."

"You kept track of him?"

"Mrs. Winter, Miss Jessica, if I may say so, was very deeply attached to her only brother, sir. It was by her instructions and for her sake, partly, that we kept ourselves informed. There was besides a business matter . . ."

Vincent now looked surly like a boy in trouble and ashamed . . . the variety of his moods manifesting themselves almost entirely in his carriage, a turn of the head, a twist of the chin or shoulders, and in his remarkably flexible voice, from which he seemed to banish life and color by will to suit his occasion.

"She wasn't so deeply attached to my mother or to me, was she?"

Manchi bowed.

"My mother rid herself of me when I was about three years old. But if she's still alive and able to read the papers, she'll be turning up at Crewe House shortly. Then we'll have a lady housekeeper, Manchi."

The valet's bow conveyed a reproof for his new master's bitter levity. Obviously he knew himself to be a more accomplished gentleman than his employer, and took a certain satisfaction in the discovery.

Vincent again jerked himself out of one of his brooding spells.

"Well, I'm going for a swim in the river, Monkey. If you want to undress and dress me, you can come along," and with that he opened the nearest French window behind him and stepped out over the tulips with apparent carelessness but, Manchi was able to observe, without so much as touching one of the juicy and fragile stalks.

Chapter 9

Sally had breakfasted in her own room, crept down to the office when Early reported that Mr. Crewe had gone out, planned for him a luncheon and a dinner which she selected from one of her mother's menu books, and then fled again to sanctuary. But when the stillness of the house and the beauty of the day, so bright and still after that tormented night, became too immediate to all her senses, she escaped stablewards and there surrendered to Jock's pleading and mounted Star. Jock accompanied her along the grassy lanes into the wood trails.

There is no finer tonic for the spirits than a horse-back ride on such a creature as Sally bestrode. Her blood came rushing back into the channels pinched by grief and shock and fear and with it, in mysterious revival, came happiness and hope. She began to envisage a golden future, her eyes grew golden to match and sparkled to the motion of the animal. Jock, watching her, felt a wistful glow.

As they came down again out of the flickering young woods into the meadows of Crewe, and by a lane into the road that led to a back farm-gate, Star gave a desperate plunge, that would have unseated a less skillful rider. "What was that?" cried Sally, her face scarlet. Jock at her side looked sharply into a nearby copse. "Some tramp or trespasser," said he and rising in his stirrups, cried wrathfully, "Hey there, come out here, you. Don't you know this is private property?"

The only answer was a rustle, an escaping step, but Sally caught a glimpse of a figure that doubled across a little opening; shabby, furtive, looking back over its shoulder with a bleached and bearded face.

"What a horrid-looking man!"

"There's plenty of 'em about these days," sighed Jock. "Not safe any longer for you to ride about alone, Miss Keyne."

When they were again in the stable yard, "I think I'll ask Mr. Crewe about the mare, Jock," said Sally, as he helped her down.

"Please do, miss. I can't believe but he'll be glad to have you own her. Which, it really seems to me, miss, you actually do."

She ran into the house by a side door and up to her own quarters, using the servants' stairway. On her tiny dressing table Early had laid a pile of letters: one from Miss Mary, two from Jane, one postmarked New Haven. This Sally opened after a pause in which her blood, her heart and pulses shared.

Robin wrote neatly in a fine formed hand so different from himself that for an instant Sally wondered if she might not be mistaken and turned to read his signature. His words, however, reassuringly declared him.

"Sally dear, I know you told me to let you write first but I can't wait. I think I'm probably out of my head but I can't think of anything but you . . . your eyes and your hair and your mouth and the way you speak. But I can't for the life of me remember your nose. It's driving me mad. Have you a nose, Sally? College is the same old grind. No, it isn't. It's a lot worse since an experience I had in Baltimore last week. I do hope you won't mind my being in love with you like this. I'm even fool enough to hope it's a sort of germ we both picked up at the St. Charles. I'm scared sick you've only got a light case.

"I hope things are going all right for you now.

"Yours . . . I honestly am beginning to believe . . . forever . . . Robin. Honest, Sally, nothing like this ever happened to me before and I'm scared. I've known lots of girls . . . some of them I guess you'd say . . . too well . . . . but this is a thing in a class all by itself. For Heaven's sake, try to join it. Try."

Sally threw herself down on her bed to laugh. But she felt as soon as she lay there extraordinarily serious and still. Here was the rescue, the golden, dancing future . . . Robin . . . Robin. . . . She pressed down her face into the pillow and there her lips shaped the memory of a kiss.

After a while she read the other letters and found beneath them a pencilled note. This was written in a labored copybook writing in pencil on a torn thin page.

"Will Miss Keyne do Vincent Crewe the favor of dining with him downstairs this evening?"

Sally gave her clock one scared look. It was already seven. She rang and sent her answer: "Please tell Mr. Crewe, Early, that I will have dinner with him downstairs this evening," then changed her mind and rang again. By the time Early returned, she was in her tub and called out, "Never mind. It was nothing . . . a . . . a mistake. Just take my message the way I said, please." She would not, she told herself, towelling fiercely, be afraid of that man. Certainly she would not show him the least degree of fear. No, if she must live in his house and take his hateful orders, at least he should be made to feel and to understand her profound spiritual independence. She was bound by no will of Caleb's, nor of Caleb's heir. She remained of her own accord, in loyalty only to her mother.

In the wardrobe of every young girl who is able to choose her own frocks there is a black dress. Housekeepers, thought Sally with one of her vigorous grimaces, always wear black. But she was entirely aware, when she looked into the mirror, that the girl in this demure sheer frock, in the sleeves of which her arms shone like netted silver fish, looked more princess than housekeeper. "A duchess with a grouch . . ." There should be no sign of grouch this evening. She would face the "tramp's" dislike with graceful nonchalance. For once, Sally rejoiced in her own fairness. There is something, she thought, much *icier* in being blonde. She wore her highest heeled slippers, schooled her mane to sleekness behind her ears. A touch of lipstick, a light mist of powder . . . she looked, she thought, glacial and assured . . . at least twenty-five years old. I wonder how old he is . . . and was startled by the notion that he might be really very young. Somehow, she had not thought of him as her contemporary, not just a youth like Robin. Vincent was thick and strong, his eyes were hard and his mouth maturely set.

Coming slowly down the stairs, she saw that he was waiting for her at its foot.

Only a short time had passed since that night when Caleb Winter's lawyer, the knowledge of a will acid on his tongue, had come down these same steps to see Caleb Winter's wife waiting beneath the hanging light. The figure of Vincent Crew had its own quality of strong and heavy patience. He too was able to wait long and well. His shadows, like hers, pointed down, making blots of his eyes, a black triangle of his mouth and sending roots through the polished floor. In Sally's mind there was no memory, of course, of that other encounter but, like Marr's, her bitter attention was fixed upon the figure in the hall.

There is a gift in which Sally believed, known as a woman's intuition. It is, in reality, the gift of every subject soul: of slave or clerk, of schoolboy, child, dog or of woman, even in her modern mitigated dependence, who watches to protect her children or herself from the moods and angers of her economic lord; a gift inspired by the arch master Fear, which once made of man a creature of hair-trigger sensitivity to sound and shadow and which all through the ages has been used by his manipulators, priest, doctor, salesman, and politico, to keep him usefully enslaved. It is the loss of this intuition through authority and protection that has given to the Junker of all nations his slow reactions, his incapacity for foresight or for comprehension of other people's emotions, a lack which so inevitably leads to his destruction. Once he has killed the watchdog Fear, extinction may creep up to his confident Lordship from any easy ambush.

This watchdog, deep in her own nerves, now put up all its hackles for Sally's benefit. She paused only an instant at sight of Crewe, waiting for her at the stairs' foot, and certainly to his eyes lost no jot nor tittle of her glacial dignity, but she was afraid. She knew, or her subconscious mind knew for her by ten thousand minute observations, that to her this man was dangerous. After that minute pause, Sally came down to his level and stood before him.

She saw that he was dressed in a new cheap blue suit

too tight for his muscular body, a pink shirt, a brown and white striped tie and a pair of tan sport shoes. She thought he had looked better in the torn khaki shirt and overalls. That horrible haircut was more noticeable and his collar seemed uncomfortably tight and as though it made his face redder than before. His expression, too, was not particularly attractive; it showed no violence of dislike but neither did it betray eagerness, softening, gratitude for her condescension in obedience.

"How is your mother?" he asked her.

She heard herself answering evenly in that silver wire voice that came to her tongue for such occasions. "She has had a paralytic stroke, Mr. Crewe, and I'm afraid her improvement will be very slow. Thank you."

Vincent got out a can of tobacco and made himself a cigarette.

"When can I get to see the old lady?" he asked.

Sally felt a heat in her face and a sort of tremble of amusement in her diaphragm.

"I don't think she can see you for a long time. She must be kept very quiet and avoid all unpleasan ... I mean, all excitement."

"Then I'd better keep out of view of her windows."

"Oh, she can't even get as far as a window yet."

"Where do you hang out?"

Sally cocked her head doubtfully.

"I mean, sleep and eat and amuse yourself ... times I'm not the joke." He had by some means discerned the hidden quiver of her laughter. "I haven't seen hide nor hair of you since our first interview."

"Mother and I have a sort of apartment at the end of the second story in the eastern wing. There's a small bedroom for me and a bigger one for her and a bath and a little sitting room. We're very comfortable."

"I'll say you are. Sounds quite homelike if you ask me. I'm supposed to turn into that four-posted tomb of old man Winter's. I slept on the sofa both nights."

"It's very comfortable," Sally murmured absentmindedly, wondering for what reason this wielder of a whip hand had decided so to veil or to mitigate his anger towards her and watching for Charles' appearance to announce the meal. If only it were over and she safe again in the rooms where she "hung out"!

Vincent shot her an eye-cornered look.

"How'd you know?"

"Know what, Mr. Crewe?"

"That the sofa in my room's so comfortable?"

Sally flushed without quite knowing why. "I slept on it the first night of my mother's illness. I had just got back from school when she was taken sick."

"I'll swap apartments with you."

She tried to laugh politely and to speak with light irony. "Thank you so much. I believe things are better as they are."

Here Charles said, "Dinner is served," and Sally swept to the place he had set for her at the table's foot. He had laid not the small drop-winged breakfast table in the window where she had eaten with her mother, but the great refectory one, narrow and a mile long, flanked by its carved empty chairs. In its centre was set a superb silver epergne holding hothouse fruit; candelabra burned six candles at either side of it.

Charles pulled back Sally's chair while the apparition-like Henry did the same for Crewe. She saw, with a faint return of her amusement, that Vincent was very deeply flushed and that he kept jerking his chin sideways in a nervous fashion. All this tremendous state was embarrassing to him but she realized that he supposed it to be the normal way of Sally's world which must now become his own, so that he was prepared to take it with what grace he could. He was following all her motions accurately, unfolding his huge embroidered napkin and taking the lid off his pottery marmite. The soup was consommé, delicately flavored. He looked up from it abruptly.

"Look a here, Miss Keyne, I'm not an invalid."

"What do you mean?"

"Well, if you're going to be my housekeeper you better come and ask me what I want to eat."

Sally sat stiff, her hands crimping the napkin on her knee.

"Oh, Mr. Crewe . . . you mean . . . my meals?"

"Sure, I mean your meals. They don't suit me for a cent."

"I . . . you were out this morning. I . . . I came down to my office in the morning after breakfast . . ."

"Where's your office?"

She described it to him carefully.

"Can I give you my orders there?"

"Of course. I suppose you can do anything you like and go anywhere you choose in your own house."

"I reckon you're right at that. Well, I can tell you here and now that I like my meals hearty and regular. Plenty of meat. And I like pastry and thick pies and cakes. I like big cups of coffee with cream and sugar with all my meals. I like hot biscuits and griddle cakes and sausages and hot dogs and pork and ham, spuds, lots of thick gravy, chicken for Sundays, ice-cream. I eat like a working man and I drink like one ... as much and as often as I can get it. That don't mean I'm a drunkard. I can quit when I've a mind to."

"I'll try to remember," said Sally. "If you will come to my office at about half-past nine or ten o'clock every morning we can plan your meals until I get to know just what you want."

Charles removed the marmites and passed French chops, green peas, mushrooms, and potato soufflé, of which Vincent seemed to make four mouthfuls.

"Where'd you go to school?" he asked apropos of nothing.

Sally told him and presently began to tell him other things. She was nervously anxious to be talkative and there was that about his poker face and still, slate-colored eyes that had the impersonal inspiration to confidence of a screened confessional. With any audience at all, Sally was apt to become eloquent on the theme of Miss Culpepper. She told Vincent Crewe the story of her school, its few enmities and many friendships, its pleasures and its annoyances, and also the tale, in part, of her vacations, those spent with Miss Mary and those in visiting. If she paused he shot out a brief inquiry or comment, "What next?" or "I'll say it was" or, "That was something."

By the time her saga began to falter, they had left the table and he had taken her to the great drawing room of their unfortunate interview. Halfway down it Sally surrendered to panic. "I think I must go up to my mother now."

"No," said Vincent, straddling the hearth beneath a portrait of his great-grandfather. "No. Look here, do you play on the piano?"

"Yes."

"Then try that one, will you? Over there near the windows. I bet it needs tuning . . . as much as we do."

As, after an instant's half-defiant hesitation, she complied, he began to pace the whole long floor from hearth to entrance door and back. So doing he passed and repassed between her and the windows, which stood open to the mildness of the night and showed a vista of trees made viridescent by the room's illumination.

Sally was made uneasy by his pacing presence. Once or twice she looked up aside, and found his eyes resting upon her without expression. She could not help feeling that during the entire rhythmic performance he kept that enigmatic look so fastened. She did not know whether she was alarmed or relieved when from the far end of his sentry walk he switched out all the lights.

She was playing without notes but stopped. "Go on," he said from that distance softly. She gave forth an uncertain sound of protest and of laughter and played again. Now, she heard him in the darkness, going sometimes on one side of the piano, sometimes on the other, his steps loud on the boards or muted on the rugs. The fragrance of his cigarette wreathed itself about her. Gradually used to the dimness she caught, by a faint emanation from the stars of early June, an outline of him, here and there, against some contrasting background, window or dimly lighted opening. Then, so monotonous became his occupation and so soothing her own, that she almost forgot him and, smiling to herself, was back with Robin in the ballroom, in the porch. Changing her tune, she played tenderly, with improvised variations, the old English melody, "What's this dull town to me? Robin's not here. What was it I wished to see? What wished to hear?"

She was startled by the abrupt cessation of Vincent's step. She could not tell where he stood until, "Don't stop suddenly," he said in a voice astonishingly near, the most carrying low voice she had ever heard, "but just come to a natural stop as soon as you can make it." She did so, and could then hear only the negroes chanting distantly and the small night sounds within and without. From this darkness his voice came again, "I thought so. Look here, Miss Sally, get up and go on out and upstairs to your own room. You won't need a light to find your way, will you?"

"No," she said doubtfully. "What's wrong?"

She leaped under his touch, an urgent grasp which he fastened upon her wrist. The hand was cold. "I heard someone outside close to these windows. Come on."

"I can see. Please let me go." He obeyed and she hurried blindly past where she thought he stood and down the room, escaping collision with the furniture by some instinct of discernment, and found herself with a sensation of relief and reassurance in the normally lighted hall. From it she fled upstairs. Looking down for an instant at the turn, she witnessed Vincent's cautious preparations for exit by the front door. Just before he switched out the hall lights, he set down his right hand into his pocket which was lumpy and sagged. He was armed! Sally waited for five minutes; her heart beat heavily. Then, with an angry and contemptuous movement of her head, went rapidly to her mother's room.

Miss Mary Culpepper had been an earnest teacher of the scriptures. Sally was reminded of a verse, "The wicked flee when no man pursueth."

She told her mother nothing of her evening except that she had had a pleasant dinner with Mr. Crewe, but, in her own bed, later, she found it for a long while impossible to sleep. She was back again in the abruptly darkened long room, up and down which went that rhythmic, haunted tread. And she was playing, like a snake charmer, afraid to stop. Annoyed at her own hectic imagination, she commanded sleep, only to be awakened at an hour of dawn. There were voices and footsteps, laughter, clatter, talk and singing down below in the great house. The devil that had gone forth so quietly into the night had brought back with him seven others louder than himself.

When she came into her office next morning, Vincent Crewe was waiting for her.

"I like this room," he said. "I think I'll take it over for my own den."

She repressed an outcry of rebellion, liking this room, herself.

"Any objections?" he demanded instantly as though she had used no repression.

She shrugged and said with careful emphasis, "I have to tell you again that it's your house, Mr. Crewe. I was thinking only that the servants are used to coming here for orders. Also, we ... I have to have some sort of workroom."

He said nothing and there fell a silence. "By the by," she sat down behind the desk and looked up at him, "would you mind telling me something?"

"I didn't find anyone in the yard last night."

"That wasn't what I meant to find out."

"Shoot."

"Where did you get that scrap of paper from, the one you used for the note asking me to come down to dinner yesterday?"

He came close, leaned opposite and stared down like a pupil baffled by his teacher's question.

"Scrap of paper? Note? Oh, sure, I get you now. I tore it out of a book in what Charles calls the 'lie-bury.' "

"I was afraid you had. I know they are your books, Mr. Crewe, but they are so beautiful, so valuable. I wish, even if you can't read them, that you ... you would learn ... sort of ... to respect them."

"Can't read them! Look here, I know how to read. I'm not so damned illiterate."

She could see by the way he turned his face aside and down that she had hurt his pride. At such an angle his blunt fixed countenance had a certain appeal.

"I didn't mean you couldn't actually read. It's only ... the way I was brought up to feel about books. No really literate person could possibly have done such a thing."

"All right. What else?"

"What else?" She was bewildered then felt the cut. "You mean, of course, that it's none of my business, that I'm impertinent. I suppose you are right. It's for you to give me instructions and criticisms, isn't it?"

He grinned. "Well, I didn't mean that but I reckon it's the truth."

"Have you thought what you'd like to eat today?"

"Sounds like feeding the animals! Sure I have. But before we begin on T-bone steak and fried potatoes, I've got a few things to ask you." He began to pace. "You've got your job all right," he said moodily, not looking at her, "but what am I going to do?"

He threw all around him, at the panelled walls, the leaf-filled windows, the pictures and the bookcases, a really desperate and astonishingly youthful look. For the first instant that she had shared with him, Sally forgot herself. She saw him not as the instrument of her mother's punishment and as her own enemy, but as a man in panic and turmoil of the soul.

"First thing I meant to do," he told her, "was to put this place on the market, sell out for whatever it would bring."

Sally had an odd sensation of feeling herself turn pale.

"Oh, no, no!"

"Why the devil not?"

"But you mustn't. You must *not*. I don't know how rich Mr. Winter was but I'm sure he has left you enough to keep up the estate."

"That's not what's eating me. I don't believe in keeping up estates."

"You're not a communist, are you?"

"No. I've been a laboring man long enough not to want any group of so-called workers to be in control of my life. I know another thing I don't want and that's a bunch of guys in colored shirts dosing me with castor oil or licking the hide off me every time I open my mouth to say what I mean. No, ma'am, if democracy can't be made to work, I think I'd like to choose me a nice old smoothie to be king and let him run the show, with the threat of an axe for his neck if he don't make me comfortable."

"So you're a Royalist," cried Sally and began to laugh in the explosive fashion of which everyone, even Sally, had always disapproved.

"I didn't know," he said, "that you had the guts to laugh like that."

Sally stopped laughing.

"What'll I do if I don't sell the place? I've got no friends here. I've had no training to be a sportsman and a gentleman. Maybe you heard the gang I brought back with me from town last night. They're not the county people that Monkey's grooming me to gang up with but they're the sort I run into in poker and billiard joints and such, the sort that's sure to fasten their suckers onto me."

"No," said Sally, "that isn't necessary. After all, you *are* a Crewe."

"I didn't ask to be one."

Sally sat straight. "Miss Culpepper used to say that the first symptom a person shows of growing up is when he accepts the reality of his own situation. I don't know how old you are . . ."

"Twenty-five," he told her.

"Is that really all?"

"You're only about sixteen."

"I'm nearly twenty."

"As old as all that comes to?"

"Well, at twenty-five you should be sort of grown up and you certainly look it. But saying you didn't ask to be a Crewe . . . why, that's as childish as saying you didn't ask to be a man or an American. You *are* a Crewe, Vincent, you can't laugh that off."

"O.K., Sally, what comes next?"

She had not realized that she had called him by his first name. His use of hers crimsoned and stiffened her. But she hurried on, not wishing to draw his attention to what she imagined was a mere slip of his tongue.

"This is all none of my business naturally."

"Sure it is. If you're going to keep house for me you got to keep me in the house."

"Well, it seems to me that the owner of such a great estate has his work cut out for him."

"Just how?"

"Have you gone around and talked to all the people that are working for you? Ernest Brunn . . ."

"Sure."

"And the stable men and the chauffeur . . . ?"

"Oh," grinned Obadiah Vincent, "George and I, as

you ought to know, have a previous acquaintance. I showed him the night life of Baltimore last week. He knows more about me even than the average guy knows about his boss and what I know about George Elmer would lose him his job with most. Only I'm not the average boss so he can stop on, that is, if he treats machinery right. I won't stand for abuse of fine machinery. That's a dandy car of yours ..." he looked completely astounded and added in a dazed voice, "I mean ... of mine," and Sally thought that for the first time he had actually realized the change in his fortunes.

"It was queer," he went on presently, "you and me meeting like that on our way down, wasn't it? A queer concatenation of circumstances." The phrase was unlike him and, for some reason, he shot a look at her when he made use of it. "Natural, of course, seeing that we were both sent for by the same party."

"Are you a trained mechanic, Mr. Crewe? Is that your profession? Is that what you've been doing?"

"I've been doing," he said, "a lot of things. At sea and on land. I've even tried being mechanic for a bunch of rum runners, good guys they were too." He stood slumped against the frame of one of the deep-silled windows. The light edged his profile. Like Mr. Marr she thought it had a predatory look, a small-headed hawk. But the body was heavy and impressive. She remembered a queer Egyptian image, hawk's head on a man's body. Osiris, was it?

Vincent, who had been thinking of the number of things he'd been doing, turned upon her now a changed and stiffened face.

"Do you know any of the nice folks round about here?" he unexpectedly demanded.

"No. That is, nobody very near."

"Can't introduce me to my neighbors, then?"

"No. But they will certainly be calling on you soon, I should think."

"Look here." He charged up again and spoke with the most profound, a positively grinding seriousness. "I kind of want to be," he turned his deepest shade of copper and blurted out the word as though it had been an indecency, "a gentleman." Instead of looking at her

for her reactions, he looked down and aside and began
to fill a blunt, old ill-smelling pipe he took out of his
pocket. "Well," he asked her, "why aren't you laughing?"

"I don't feel like laughing. I like what you said."

"*Do* you? Well, look here, you was brought up and
educated to be the boss of this establishment and now
you're *out*. I was brought up to be a thug or a gangster
or at best a kind of wage-earning tramp, and I'm *in*.
Suppose you earn your board and keep by passing me
on some of the education which had ought by rights to
have been mine."

Sally felt breathless but was spared the effort of answering by a ringing of the desk telephone. Vincent instantly took up the receiver.

"Hullo, who you say you want?"

Sally saw him crimson and knew that the crisp
speaker on the wire had addressed him as a servant
who has forgotten his telephone manners.

"I hear you! I get you! Maybe you don't know it but
you want to speak to Mr. Crewe's housekeeper. Well,
there ain't any other Miss Keyne. No, nor any other
Miss Sally Keyne. Mr. Crewe's housekeeper," said
Vincent, speaking through his teeth, "is not at liberty to
take a personal phone message until after her working
hours . . . say about six P.M." And he hung up.

He turned sideways and stood still, looking down. He
must have felt Sally's fury which had made her speech-
less. She suffered a throbbing in her temples and a
strange weakness in her wrists.

"Who . . ." She had to stop and control her breath.
"Who . . . was it . . . that asked to speak to me?"

"How do I know? I didn't get his name. One of your
boy friends likely." He moved away and sought the
shelter of the deep-silled leaf-clouded windows. "I told
him off like that for two reasons. I didn't like his speak-
ing-voice, which I reckon I've heard before." Then it
was Robin Ashe! "And I didn't want him to think he
could interrupt my business, not in that tone of voice!"

"Mr. Crewe, you will never be a gentleman!"

At that he merely narrowed his hard eyes and tightened his hard mouth.

"I don't believe . . . I think I shall have to explain . . . I mean . . . I am sure you don't understand my position in this house."

"Sure I understand it. You're here on sufferance."

"What on earth do you mean?"

"I mean you got no legal right to the shelter of this roof. I mean, I can throw you out any day or any minute of any day I darn please."

She stood up and leaned down on both her hands, as her mother had stood and leaned to see the written words of her disaster.

She felt her mouth and tongue and throat go dry. It was the truth. She had not so far realized it. In that will of Caleb Winter's, no provision had been made for Isabel Winter's child by her first husband. Under the spur of her necessity she had thought of herself not as an independent entity but as a substitute. She was acting as her mother's alter ego, to save for her a home and a livelihood. But the truth was—the reality she must now be mature enough to accept—that she had no right whatever in her own person here at Crewe House and that she could fill the difficult position of Crewe's housekeeper only, as he had expressed it, by his sufferance.

"Well," he said, "now you got something wished on *you* and let's see how grown up you are going to be about it."

Sally moved her pale young lips carefully. She had the look of a child's illness on her face.

"I am going to take is as maturely as I can, Mr. Crewe. You are perfectly right of course. I'm not thinking of myself." The edges of her lips grew fine and sharp and he saw that beautiful darkening of her eyes for tears. "I am thinking of . . . Mother."

Vincent spoke roughly. "Go on up to her now. I'll write down my bill of fare and give it to Charles. You got no need to worry . . . yet. I want you right now more than you ever wanted anyone in all your life, I reckon. You will earn your board and keep." And, with that, he touched her on her shoulder as lightly as though she had been charged with some deadly current. Sally laughed and felt a rush of tears. Through them she gave him an enormous and uncertain look and ran away.

She ran almost into Charles who, with trouble in his own little wrinkled face, approached the office door.

"Is Mr. Crewe in there, Miss Sally, ma'am?"

"Yes, Charles." She had controlled her tears and turned her face aside.

"There's a man here I got to let to see him."

The man, to whom Charles' furtive gesture now directed her attention, stood just inside the door of the entrance at the far end of the hall, a curious and vaguely shocking figure, blanched and bleached, insolent, timid and old. These things Sally could see in one tear-disturbed look.

"I don't think, Charles," she admonished softly, "you should let such people into the house at all."

"No, miss. I'm agreeable to that my own self. But he just forced the door. He'd git past me no matter what and I reckon I better face him with Mister Crewe himself."

"I think you had."

Sally went up the stairs but, glancing back once at the dubious intruder, saw that he was looking up at her through a dingy blanched forelock with such a speculative look as chilled her flesh. She wondered if perhaps it had been this shape, moving among the trees, that had scared Star off the wood trail and had made that step which had drawn Vincent out with a heavy right-hand pocket into the night.

"A man's past," thought Sally sententiously as a school girl or boy so often thinks, being primed with quotations, "is a trap for his future."

But her own future, innocent of anything that might be called a Past, was baited with every sort of fear. Let her master touch her shoulder with that thick, red, hateful hand of his and reassure her with his soft, rough-worded voice, she had, all the more for his moment of compunction, that sensation of a slave.

She would not go to her mother with the stigmata of tears, but in her own room she managed to compose herself. She reread Miss Mary's letter. "If you meet with anything you can't work out safely for yourself, dear Sally, you must come straight to me." Here was comfort.

"Miss Mary darling," said her pupil mournfully, "I may have to call on you for a rescue. It isn't going to be anything like a safe road for me, not any of the way."

Chapter 10

If Cinderella, returned from her ball to disenchantment, had written a letter to her handsome Prince, the document would have been very much like that which Sally wrote to Robin Ashe. He did not telephone to Mr. Crewe's housekeeper, at six P.M. or later, as she had half-feared, half-hoped he would, but for this omission she easily excused him. He had already written and was owed an explanation of her circumstances.

So now, on a morning of threatening rain, she wrote, dramatizing her situation as youth must, and certainly with some excuse! and feeling towards him as proud and as timid, as trustful and as dubious, as Cinderella might herself have felt. In this letter, Obadiah Vincent Crewe certainly filled the rôle of a wicked step-relation, and even received credit for a sort of sinister intention which the writer had not intended or did not herself discern. More of her fear and anger towards him, her sense of psychic helplessness was betrayed than she had any notion of herself. "He has me in his power," wrote Cinderella. "I'm entirely dependent. I can't do anything." Sally was an eloquent writer, having a gift for word pictures. No man of the knightly age or temperament could have read her account of herself unmoved. No man obsessed by the beauty of her eyes could have read it without a tumult of the heart. Upon Robin Ashe its effect was fairly catastrophic; nor was his family long left unaware of the volcanic influence. The result was a disturbed breakfast in the home of Mr. and Mrs. Ronald Ashe.

The home, like Sally's, was theirs by sufferance, its real owner being Ronald's widowed and wealthy sister, Heather Gayle. This lady sat at the head of her own table, her brother and sister-in-law on either side, and showed above her silver coffee urn the face of gentle feminine tyranny. Mrs. Gayle always said good morning cheerfully; in fact she said good morning three times cheerfully and then, putting on a pair of bowed Oxford glasses above a short sharp nose, she minutely examined the family mail which by her command was always put at her place and left there undisturbed until she had looked over it. Today she said, first: "If you don't pay that dentist bill at once, Milly dear ... you are so girlishly carefree about bills, aren't you? ... I suppose I shall have to attend to it and deduct the amount from some other portion of the family budget." And second: "Why, here's a letter from Robbie, addressed to both of you. That suggests a communication of some importance. Do you suppose, by any remote chance, that the boy has again exceeded his allowance?"

Mrs. Gayle was far more indulgent to her nephew, provided he remained within the general paddock of her intentions, than she had ever been with any other living soul since the sudden death of her handsome young husband many years ago. So Robin's mother was not unduly alarmed. She opened the letter, Ronald merely giving it one hungry and gentle look. He was a small boyish man with a tiny grey moustache perched on a small puckered and unhappy mouth and a little grey cockscomb of curls on his round head. His eyes, too, were round, scared and ready to be pleased. He was very nattily dressed in clothes that he had bought carefully and used even more carefully for many seasons. Robin's mother was beautiful and had, as Sally surmised, bestowed upon Robin and a daughter recently released from Heather's tyranny by a successful marriage, her lovely narrow head, sloping eyes and sly, enchanting smile. The shape of this smile, evoked as usual for her husband's benefit, faded as she read her Robin's letter.

Robin wrote with that intense reasonableness and plausibility of youth announcing revolution, that he intended with their consent to leave college and had planned to use the money Aunt Heather had so generously promised for his education here and in Europe for an early marriage to a young woman named Sara Keyne now living at Crewe House, "the famous Crewe House," and who was "just the sort of girl both you and Auntie will adore. I can get a situation as draughtsman in Mr. Molton's office if you and Dad will use your pull and then work my way up. Auntie's money will be ample to keep me and Sally going for a year or two and, I dare say, the good old girl will stand for helping us out a bit then if it should still be necessary . . . considering she hasn't any children of her own and has always been so fond of me. This depression is about over now and by next year there will be a regular boom in building . . . etc., etc., etc."

Millicent Ashe read and the brain behind her narrow brow worked rapidly. She too had a well-developed woman's intuition. Before Heather had time to put out her slender acquisitive hand, Millicent began to read the letter aloud. She read rather slowly as though Robin's writing were not so legible as usual and what she read was a confusing chronicle of college happenings, sport and study and students' gossip. "That's the dullest letter we've ever had from Robin," said Millicent and, crumpling up the closely covered sheets, she tossed them into the little open fire that crackled superfluously in the already sun-warmed room.

"Milly!" cried Ronald before he caught her look.

Heather sat back sharply in her chair. "I should have liked to read Robin's letter."

Millicent made what looked like an attempt to rescue the burning papers. "How stupid of me. I am so sorry, Heather. But it was such a dull letter that it made me cross. Besides, I'd read it out to you."

It was rarely easy for Millicent to arrange a private interview with her husband but eventually that morning she did succeed, without rousing Heather's suspicion of an unusual event, in getting him to herself in their own bedroom and there, sotto voce, she confided the true contents of Robin's letter and the fact of her dismay.

"I simply don't dare to breathe a word of this to Heather," she cried, her face quite aged and broken.

"He's perfectly and completely and unutterably mad," said Ronald Ashe. "Of course we mustn't breathe a word to Heather. She'd be rabid. What will you write to Rob?"

"I can't understand him. He's always been so sort of cold about girls." Robin's parents knew nothing of the girls Robin might perhaps have been said to "know too well." "This thing must have struck him like a thunderbolt. It does explain that queer flying visit of his, doesn't it? He'll get over it of course but meanwhile . . ."

"I'll send him a wire," said Ronald who had been pulling at his moustache. " 'Plan absurdly impossible. Use your head. Money available only for original purpose.' Something of that sort. And you write to him, will you, Milly? And just tell him where he gets off. I thought he had a better sense of reality. He ought to know his aunt after all these years. Hazel would never . . ."

"Never mind what your perfect daughter Hazel would never do. Listen, Ronnie, why don't you go over to Crewe House and cast your eye on the girl. Find out something about her?"

"Why don't I? How in Heaven's name can I get the car for a visit to Crewe House? Of all places. You've forgotten a certain chapter of family history, haven't you, Mill? You don't remember our *cause célèbre* . . . Heather's husband . . . my brother-in-law's extramarital affair with Jessica Crewe? He was about to get a divorce from Heather to marry Jessica when his car slipped off the road . . ."

"Oh, I *had* forgotten. That makes it worse. Is this girl a Crewe?"

"I reckon she must be. I'm a bit vague about the family now. Did a Crewe marry a Keyne? I can't remember."

Millicent wrinkled her forehead and closed her charming eyes.

"Jessica married an old Yankee with money, named . . . wait a sec . . . Summer? Fall? . . . No, Winter. Caleb Winter. Did they have any children? But, of course, the name wouldn't be . . . or was it Caleb Keyne? That would sound sort of wintry . . . 'Thy tooth is not so keen.' The worst of these associative memory systems is that there are too many clues. Caleb married again some woman he'd kept ... oh well, that's what they always say about widowers' housekeepers ... years ago. But of course Jessica had a brother. Any Crewe brother's child, though, would be named Crewe. ... Well, I give it up. But I've simply got to see the girl somehow. I tell you what. I can get Hazel to come and take me over for one of the Visiting Days. It would be Thursday, I think, wouldn't it? Heather needn't know where we're going."

Said Ronald gloomily, "I'll have to stay here and go out with Heather, then, in your place."

Thursday was Visiting Day at Crewe House, which, on such days, was thrown open as to its grounds and certain of its rooms, to the Public. A charge of twenty-five cents per visitor was collected at a temporary table set up in the front hall by Charles and to Manchi, eloquent and obsequious, was delegated the conducting of visitors and the patter of description and historic fact.

The family kept itself in seclusion.

On the following Thursday there was an unusual crowd of sightseers. The story of the hobo heir and the disinherited widow provided a sort of unspoken spice to Manchi's discourse.

Amongst the motor tourists and the local curiosity mongers, there were two ladies who immediately enlisted the respect of Charles and of Manchi and to whom the latter addressed the greater portion of his remarks. They were very much alike, a mother and a daughter, the young woman taller, narrower, more smartly dressed although the lesser in beauty and distinction. They had entered their names as required in the visitors' book where Charles read, "Mrs. Ronald Ashe and Mrs. Ernest Vintry." County families, he thought, and they should be leaving cards on Mr. Crewe.

Manchi, entering the upstairs hall, opened the door of a formal, meticulously ordered bedroom. "Here it was that General Tarleton of the British army was quartered with his officers at the time when, surprised by a rumor of Revolutionary troops, he rode his horse up the great stairs of Crewe House, as I shall describe to you presently as we go down again into the hall."

The tourists bunched themselves inconveniently in the room and refrained from touching the furniture and ornaments. Mrs. Vintry, who had lingered near the door, caught at her mother's elbow. "Wait here a second—Mother. Look! Down towards the end of this passage! Quick!"

A girl stood, remote, unaware of observers, a girl in a blue linen frock beside an open window. She was signalling to someone below her in the grounds. They could hear her swift warm urgent voice. "Yes, Jock . . . I think so . . . in about an hour. I want to speak to *him* about Star first."

The girl was lightly built and moved with fluency. Her tawny hair glittered in the window's light. She turned and they saw her big-eyed dreaming face.

"Ask the guide," hissed Robin's sister.

Manchi returned to the threshold and looked where Mrs. Ashe directed him.

"Is that by any chance a Miss Sally Keyne, guide?"

"Yes, madam," said Manchi. "Yes. That is certainly Miss Keyne, if you please, madam."

Here Sally saw them and saw that she was the object of their attention. Her bright young color flashed into her face, she lifted her head, gave them one proud cloistered look and then advancing, moved with her gallant grace into one of the rooms along the passage and closed the door.

"Who is she, guide? Such a pretty creature! I mean, what relation is she to the master of the house?"

Manchi's pale face and prominent eyes betrayed no malice. Perhaps the form his information took was purely accidental. He came up close and smiled and lowered to confidence his half-British, half-native voice. "Why, madam," said Manchi and blew forth that cloud no bigger than a man's hand that grew to the overcasting of Sally's firmament, "she came here only a few days ago at the time of the change, madam. We calls her, here in the house, Mr. Crewe's housekeeper . . . by courtesy, as it were, madam."

Then, as though aware of evil, he drew back, turned to his other followers and raised his key. "Our next visit is to the room occupied by a lady who refused to marry two of the greatest of American statesmen, General George Washiongton and Mr. Thomas Jefferson. And I have a quaint ghost story to tell apropos of her rejection when we come to one of our downstairs sitting rooms. . . . If you please, ladies and gentlemen."

Mrs. Vintry and Mrs. Ashe moved forward with the rest and appeared to be attentive listeners. But the face of the one was scarlet, and of the other pale; the eyes of Millicent carried a look of grief and shock while Hazel's held a bitter little smile of cynicism.

Chapter 11

The cloistered look did not last Sally beyond the door of her escape from the observation of Mrs. Vintry and of Mrs. Ashe. Inside the linen room, for that was her unromantic sanctuary, she stood with all her pulses in disorder and her face on fire. For she had instantly recognized Robin's mother and sister, their resemblance to him being unmistakable, and she was torn by the conviction that they had come to spy upon her, to investigate her situation and to draw conclusions wounding to her pride. From her distance, Manchi's look and gesture had seemed patently contemptuous.

In order to make assurance sure, she went—as soon as the tourists had left Crewe House—to inspect the Visitors' Book and there, of course, they were set down: Mrs. Ronald Ashe and Mrs. Ernest Vintry. Why had they come like this and not left cards on her mother and Mr. Crewe, if not on her insignificant self? Was it merely an accidental visit, not inspired by any mention from Robin of a certain Sally Keyne?

She stood in her blue linen frock, entirely forgetful of the prospective ride with Jock and of the interview she had planned with Vincent Crewe, frowning down upon the small memorandum book while Charles picked up his table and booklets and cash box.

Vincent, himself, emerging from her workroom into the hall where she bent over the signatures, here accosted her.

"You're the guy I want to see," he said, avoiding her eyes and speaking with his usual soft surliness. "Come in here a minute, will you?"

It was evident that her anger over his interference

with Robin's telephone communication was to be ignored. As usual Sally first hesitated and then complied.

"I wanted to see you too," she said.

In the workroom it was Vincent, this time, who seated himself behind the desk where stood the instrument of their recent quarrel, the small black gnome of telephone magic. She saw that Vincent had been writing or reading there. He really did intend to take possession of her own private corner on the ground floor of the house! Sally betook herself to the deep-silled, green-shadowed window.

"I wanted," she said, "to ask you about a horse."

"That's another one of those queer concatenations of event," said Vincent, "because that's just what I was going to ask you."

"You see, my mother, before Mr. Winter's will was read, had bought me a mare."

"Yes?"

"Well ... if I can arrange to pay for her feed and care ..."

Vincent interrupted her. "Wait until I've given you my point of view about riding horses! I seem to own a stable. About six blooded critters with high heads and proud hearts and what I don't know about equestrianism would make Godfrey and Jock Nunn seasick. How about me selling the whole outfit?"

She thought it strange that he should feel this compulsion to ask her opinion as to any proposed sale of his new property.

"Don't you want to ride, Mr. Crewe?"

"Monkey is going up to New York to buy me golf pants and riding pants and ballroom pants and cocktail pants and parlor croquet pants. I thought maybe I could cut down on one item of my wardrobe."

"You ought to ride. It would be good," said Sally with one of her sudden attacks of ruthlessness, "for your figure."

He jerked back his shoulders. "What's wrong with my figure?"

"It's too heavy ... sort of ..."

He stood up and looked down at himself. She saw that he was admirably narrow of hips and lean of waist.

Scarlet, she hurried on, "What I mean is . . . a . . . a riding figure is . . . in a way . . . a gentleman's figure. I mean . . . you know, a . . . a cavalier . . ."

He sat down and back and stared.

"So you think I got to ride to get the shape of a gentleman?"

"Not exactly. I mean . . . it's one of the things a . . . a Virginian gentleman can do."

"Sure. O.K. Come on out and give me a riding lesson. If you use your horse . . ."

"She's a mare."

"That's all right with me. If you use your mare for riding out with me, it's fair enough for me to feed her. If you're my riding teacher . . ."

Sally, startled, came out from her niche.

"Haven't you ever ridden really?"

"A mule . . . coupla times."

"These horses are . . . might be . . . a little high life for a beginner."

"Oh, I might as well get spilled sooner as later. You know all there is to know about riding, don't you?"

"Gracious no. But I've ridden all my life. I took riding and jumping lessons for years and I've hunted a little. I even gave riding lessons a few times at school when the regular master was away."

He stared at her now gloomily.

"Seems a shame they didn't look me up and give me just a few of the teachings you got. Well, I reckon I've got to get my education to be the heir, second hand. Let's go."

He stood up from the desk.

"You ought to get some breeches and boots."

"Manchi goes north any day now, but, till he gets back, there's a whole rig of that sort in the closet back of my suite. I guess it must have belonged to old Winter when he was spring. Or else maybe to my father when he was a kid here. Anyway, I can get into it . . . even if I haven't a gentleman's figure.

"And, look here, before we get out for my first ride, which maybe will be my last, I want you should give me a list of books I ought to kind of catch up on for an education and . . . and I read something here in this poetry book that I want to read out to you because it sure is a picture of you."

Sally, at this, simply looked at him with all the greatness of her multi-colored, her almost rainbow eyes.

He had taken up his "poetry book" where it lay on its face and now "read out" to her carefully:

"With thy clear keen joyaunce
Languor cannot be.
Shadow of annoyance
Never came near thee:
Thou lovest but ne'er knew love's sad satiety."

She felt breathless.

"A . . . picture of me, Mr. Crewe?"

"Sure. I know well enough you've had sorrow and worries just lately but 'joyaunce' don't mean just the same as being happy and . . . 'shadow of annoyance' is just something that don't fasten onto you. It's a heap different from being mad all through the way you get sometimes. About the loving . . . of course . . . I reckon you're in love now this minute and I reckon it's for the first time and I reckon I know who the feller is. But you have never known" . . . and, turning down and aside his expressionless hard eyes he repeated in a voice so full of feeling that it made her nerves contract . . . "love's sad satiety." "That last," he said, banishing the plangent, searching note, "is a word I had to look up in a dictionary."

Sally, after one long, blinking and bewildered look, fairly fled from him.

"I am going to change into riding clothes," she called downstairs . . . for he had followed her, as though automatically, out into the hall. "I'll meet you at the stables. Jock has saddled two horses. He . . . we . . . we were just going out for a ride."

She reached the stables first and prepared Jock for his new master's intention. The boy's face fell.

"Then you'll be riding with him, won't you, Miss Sally?"

Sally laughed with a malice of her own.

"I reckon Mr. Crewe will have enough after his first

ride on Plucky to last him for a fortnight, Jock, if not forever."

But in this prophecy, which at the moment brightened Jock, Sally was utterly mistaken.

With his heavy jaw tight set, Vincent got himself into the saddle while Jock, ironic amusement in his eyes, held the restive animal. Sally was already up. She gave Vincent a few instructions, as to his seat and reins; Jock let go Plucky's head, and both horse and rider became instantly a diminishing motion picture haloed in sunset dust.

When Sally overtook the rider, perhaps half an hour later, he was mounting a steep hill and seemed, though copper-colored and bathed in sweat, to be not only firmly seated but in strong, if awkward control of his beast. He was no doubt breaking every rule of a cavalier's code but he was still astride. Sally could see the gripping strength of his back and thighs and, all through the figure, the fury of the man's will and pride. She knew that not if Plucky should stand on his head or leap over the little new moon visible above the trees, would he be able to rid himself of his sinewy master.

There was not much conversation between pupil and instructor on this first ride, Sally merely ejecting a few obvious reminders, "Don't ride him on the bit, get the feel of his mouth in your hands." But, "I think," she said as they returned to the stables, "that you are a natural horseman, Mr. Crewe." He looked down and aside, saying nothing.

Jock, at their bridles, repressed a grimace.

"So you managed to stick him, sir?"

Flinging himself suddenly to the ground, Vincent grinned and set his hard grey look upon the boy.

"Disappointed?"

Jock reddened. "Why no, sir. I'm just a bit surprised like. What I mean ... I hadn't thought you were a rider."

"I'm not. I'm just a blasted leech. Look here, Jock. Miss Keyne and I will be riding again every afternoon now at half-past three o'clock."

Sally's color rose but she would not fan the quick blue fire of revolution in Jock's eyes.

"I've promised to give Mr. Crewe riding lessons,

Jock. Perhaps you can help me out sometimes when you have nothing to do."

No sooner, however, were they out of earshot than Vincent, striding as though his legs were not quite under control, said sullenly, "He damn well can't."

Sally did not understand.

"Jock damn well can't help you out. You're in, Miss Sally, into this job of making me a gentleman. I kind of reckon you're in for a longer sentence than you know . . . maybe, for life."

She did not ask him this time what he meant. Her heart was cold with prophecy. That night she wrote to Miss Mary Culpepper her first admission of genuine personal dismay.

"I don't know what he wants of me. I don't feel he really hates me any more . . . and yet . . . there is a coldness and an irony about his confidences that seem to hide an ugly feeling. It's as if he enjoyed having me in his power, knowing that I don't dare fly out at him or run away. If it weren't for Mother I'd come straight to you."

She was seated at the little table in her own bedroom and looked up from her signature at the sound of a knocking.

"Come in."

It was Vincent at her door.

The little silver clock her mother had given her with Caleb Winter's money ticked away from eleven o'clock.

Sally stood up.

"Mr. Crewe! Is . . . is anything wrong?"

He was deeply flushed.

"I've just been in to visit with your mother," he told her slowly in a voice of indecipherable emotion, entirely absent from his face. "I just want to tell you that I didn't do her any harm. We had a fine talk. Miss Sally," his eyes were set upon her with almost defiant expressionlessness, "your mother is a great lady. I don't wonder any more at you putting up with misery on her account. By Judas," said Vincent, "I feel like I could do a lot of unlikely things for her, myself."

He stepped back, having advanced only one step into her room, and shut the door.

It was like an apparition or ... or a cuckoo clock. What a sudden queer animal he was!

She hurried, as soon as she was certain he had left their part of the house, into her mother's room. The bed light still burned, throwing its light across her patient hands. She was propped high on her pillows. The slight distortion of paralysis was still perfectly visible in lid and mouth and trailing arm, but the woman's natural vigor had now repossessed her quick dark glance and strong regular face. She smiled sidelong at Sally, showing her splendid teeth.

"Mother darling, I told him to keep away."

After a long silent upward look Mrs. Winter said, "We're lucky, aren't we?"

Sally felt an assault of blood to her face.

"Did ... did you like him?" She tried to banish incredulity out of her voice.

"He told me," Mrs. Winter smiled, "that you do *not.*"

"Oh, Mother!"

Mrs. Winter looked amused. "Of course that's natural." She stared up at the girl's bewildered, struggling face, then pressed her fingers hard and dropped them.

"Never mind. Don't be worried. I know I ought to hate him. If you had lived my life," she turned her head a little aside, "you'd be grateful for small mercies."

Sally's throat ached with an ache that had become painfully familiar. "But, darling, do you think Vincent Crewe is even a small mercy?" Her lips curled unpreventably.

At that Mrs. Winter laughed and said, "He's very young. And so are you. Put out the light, Sally. I'm going to sleep well tonight."

Sally kissed her and obeyed. But she was herself far from the tranquillity of sleep. There was now fear in the very heart of her one sanctuary. Vincent had undermined her there. What was his purpose? What could he intend? Some special delicacy of punishment. The whip hand had gloved itself first and then put out of sight its ugly weapon. But she knew in all her nerves, even without recalling the insults and unkindness of her actual experience with him, the deadly power of sustained emotion this man possessed. He relished her helplessness and did not mind stooping to increase it. One by one he was stripping from her her poor defences. It was partly, she imagined, a matter of class feeling. Once she had drawn aside her skirts and shrunk away from him. Now, it was his especial gratification to tread, to press close, closer, so that her very physical being was not exempt from his increasing proximity. He had taken his place at her desk, he had stood beside her mother's sickbed, he had even entered into her little bedroom. Was there no possible escape? She would ask Joseph Marr. It might be that she could borrow money, could get a position as teacher from Miss Mary at St. Sylvester's, could repay the loan. It was necessary for her to escape from Crewe House, out of Vincent Crewe's power, which, as day followed day, became more and more obvious and absolute.

Behind closed lids in the darkness of her bed, she saw him astride of the rebellious horse, mastering him awkwardly and strongly ... "just a blasted leech."

Terribly oppressed, the girl turned on her light and took up a book from her bed table. But even this companion of solitude had now its association. Pushing back her tawny mane with a gesture of desperate confusion, she heard his beautiful voice reading out carefully and slowly:

> *"With thy clear keen joyaunce*
> *Languor cannot be.*
> *Shadow of annoyance*
> *Never came near thee.*
> *Thou lovest but ne'er knew love's sad satiety."*

"Oh when," wailed Sally, throwing down her book and herself with desperation against her pillow, "when will Robin write?"

Chapter 12

No sooner had he received his father's telegram, "Use your head. Plan absurdly impossible. Money available only for original purpose," and his mother's letter, written before her visit to Crewe House and telling him, with the mitigation of a mother's tenderness, "where to get off," than Robin fell back upon the second defence line of his planned campaign. He appeared at Fallows, his Aunt Heather's home, at three o'clock of a June afternoon.

This hour was fortunately one of Heather Gayle's napping, so that Ronald and Millicent were able to bootleg their errant son into their own apartments practically unobserved.

"Well," said Ronald, trying to be stern and remembering parental clichés, "what is the meaning of this? And what have you got to say for yourself?"

"I've made up my mind," said Robin, unnaturally white about the lips and incandescent of dark eyes, "and all I want, Mother and Dad, is for you to be loyal, to back me up."

"We are loyal to your best interests, Robin."

In spite of her perturbation, Millicent was able to enjoy the glow of her pride in this handsome resolute young man who stood against their bedroom mantel, wearing his grey travelling suit so well, looking, in spite of love and desperation, so crisp and clean and finely groomed. Robin was born, she thought, with that strange gift of correctness, had worn his very bonnets and bootees with an air of distinction.

"Mother darling, I have to be the judge of my own interests. You forget that I am twenty-three years old."

"It's difficult to remember when you go off your head like this."

Vibrant and rigid all through his long lithe body, Robin turned on the speaker. "Dad, don't say that. I'm not in the least degree off my head. I've found the girl I am going to marry. That's not childish and it's not insane. The fact that we're poor and dependent upon Aunt Heather is not my fault, is it?"

Ronald turned aside while Millicent said softly, "No, dear, it's not your fault," and there came a pause of pain, reproach and slow mutual anger.

"You see, Mother and Dad, this is something I just can't help. Of course if you can't wangle enough money out of Aunt Heather to make it possible for me to marry . . ."

"Now listen to me, Robin, and hold your tongue a minute. Nobody's going to wangle money for you to marry anyone. You've got to finish your college course and get yourself prepared to make a living. We don't enjoy dependence any better than you do and why you should deliberately plan to start your life in the position of a dependent with your mother's and my situation so vividly before you, is more than I can understand. I said to myself after the war when we lost our money and when my condition prevented me from holding down a job, if there's one thing I'm going to give my son, it's the means of earning his own livelihood. Well, that's been provided, at a cost you can't realize, and, before I let you throw away the most precious, the most essential gift a man can have, I'll see this girl of yours . . ."

"Hush, Ronnie. I know all about the girl."

"What do you mean?" Robin's color laid itself as with a full brush, crimson across his cheekbones. "Know all about Sally?"

"Yes, dear." It was a sad breath.

"Well, isn't she the most wonderful . . . isn't she worth flunking out of Yale for?"

This caused a sort of thunderous diversion. Robin, it appeared, upon receipt of his parents' expression of opinion . . . "which sounded absolutely final, if you ask me" . . . had gone into his June exams with the deliberate intention of failure. "Of course I won't hear until

July or August, but I didn't take any chances. There's hardly a question I didn't manage to answer wrong."

After a deadly stillness like the one at the centre of a hurricane, "All right, my boy," said Ronald hoarsely, "you get into your car with me and we go straight back to New Haven and there, if wangling means anything at all, I'll wangle another set of examination papers and you will pass or . . ."

"Or what, Dad?"

"Or," Ronald fairly uprooted his moustache, "or take a position behind a counter in some store next week."

"Robin darling! Ronald, hush! Why do you waste all this anger and these silly threats? If only you'd let me tell him. Robin, darling, I'm so sorry for you."

She came from her miserable perch on the side of her bed and put up both her slim hands, folding them behind tall Robin's neck. He kissed her warmly, eagerly, with one of his endearing looks.

"Dear Mother, you're such a darling. Let's begin all over again. We three mustn't fight, we've always got along."

"Yes, honey. But Ronald, go on out, will you? and keep Heather busy when she comes down. Tell her I've got a headache and you drive out with her. Now, Robin dear, sit down with me and listen and be patient and don't take out anything that hurts you on me, will you, sweet? Because I do love you and I'm your mother."

"Go on, Mother. You can't say anything to hurt me very awfully."

"But I'm afraid I can. I saw your pretty Sally."

"Did you? Honest? Mother, isn't she a beautiful thing?"

"Yes, dear. I saw her at the end of a hall with the sun on her hair. I asked a guide . . . it was Visitors' Day at Crewe House and Hazel and I were going through it. We . . . we thought we'd better just . . ."

"Why didn't you call on her?"

This Millicent ignored. "We asked the guide to tell us who she was."

"Well, *Mother!* You aren't . . . you can't be such a snob! Do you know the poor kid's fix? Do you know why she is keeping house for that unutterable bounder?

That cad who has inherited millions and yet forces her to stay and work for him because . . ."

"Hush, dear. The guide said . . ." Millicent looked away, holding tightly both of his hands. "The guide said, 'She came here just at the time of the change. We call her, here in the house, Mr. Crewe's housekeeper . . . by *courtesy*.' "

Robin for a minute sat perfectly still, then he drew away his hands and stood up and lit a cigarette. The match shook. He did not speak for a long minute then his voice was quiet.

"The low-down dirty cur!" he said.

"Robin!"

"Excuse me, Mother. I won't stop to talk this over with you. I'm sort of at the end of my rope. I'd say things I'd be sorry for. Just this . . . Sally came to Crewe House from St. Sylvester's School. You get that, don't you?"

"Not that tone to me, please, Robin!"

"St. Sylvester's School. You might write to Miss Culpepper . . . you've heard of Miss Culpepper, haven't you? . . . for a reference. Sally came from school at the time of her stepfather's death."

"Who?"

"Caleb Winter was her stepfather. Her mother is his widow. Naturally Mrs. Winter expected . . ."

"Oh, of course, I know about the will, but . . . I didn't know . . ."

"You didn't know that Mrs. Caleb Winter had been married before and that Sally was her daughter. You just took it for granted that your son was such an ignorant boob that he'd pick up a . . . a tramp's girl . . ."

"Robin. Robin. Robin . . ."

". . . and fall for her and want to marry her. No, I can't stay here and talk to you now. I'll go to Hazel . . ."

"Please! Please!"

He had caught up his coat, hat and valise and was gone, running down the stairs with that expert unthinking speed of youth and was gone out of the front door of Fallows. Millicent heard his car depart.

After a while, "Thank Heaven, I don't think Heather saw or heard. It's better for him to go to Hazel. She'll know how to handle him," Millicent decided, and went to bathe her face clear of all traces of trouble but those faint lines that had been etched deeper by this fiery hour.

By the time Robin in his dusty roadster came out on the southern highway that afternoon it was past five o'clock. The sky was pied, June blue and thunder black. Turning towards Hazel Vintry's house, as far north of Hanbury as the Gayle house was south of it, Robin faced the thunder blackness and was unconsciously pleased by it and its white racing storm-spray, since it was congenial to his own mood. He had not often been angry with his lovely mother and now he fancied that he hated her and the poison of such unnatural hatreds made acid of his blood. He was talking to himself so that his whitened lips moved across set teeth.

Presently he was able to concentrate his anger upon Crewe as the cause of Millicent's blundering insult to Sally. "I'll take that infernal cad out and horsewhip him," was Robin's final decision, a relieving one because he could not so much as imagine thrashing either of his gentle parents.

Some miles beyond Hanbury the storm in his blood met the storm in the air, which came with such a tearing rush of wind and lightning-silvered rain that Robin perforce first stopped his engine by the blind roadside and then, catching windy glimpses of stone gateposts surmounted by an arched sign, "Grassways Inn," crept between them and came to shelter in a porte-cochere of the building.

He entered, bent upon ordering himself a drink of some sort and waiting over it until the worst of the storm should be passed. It was now dinner time and the cocktail he sipped before a fireplace filled with blossoming dogwood branches made him hungry. In the Inn dining room, sparsely occupied, he ate a hearty meal and found himself reassured and steadied by his own gastronomic pleasure. Grassways Inn had a good cook and its service, though somewhat unnerved by lightning and thunder, was cordial, pretty and quick.

Robin smoked a cigarette over his demitasse and decided that his plight wasn't so tragic after all. By now his mother would be repentant and ashamed. That bit of information about St. Sylvester's would have done its work, as well as the knowledge of Sally's right to be in Caleb Winter's house. Millicent had acted rashly under a false belief so he had no just reason for his fury at her mistake. So much for Millicent! His father was simply the kindest and most manageable of men. Robin could work him over in no time while, as for Auntie, she'd always doted on him. Chances were she'd come round. All that Robin and Sally now needed was determination, good humor, patience and a complete mutual understanding. The quickest way to arrive at the last was for Robin and Sally to get together and outline their campaign. The course of true love, quoth Robin, surprised at his own literary knowledge—was it Shakespeare or the Bible?—never did run smooth. He'd maybe just spend the night here at Grassways Inn and then, after breakfast, go to Crewe House and have a thorough understanding with Sally before he approached Hazel at all. Maybe he could just take Sally to Hazel, get her away from Vincent Crewe.

A vision of this "understanding" made the young man dream, sent a glow into his handsome face and eyes. He betook himself to a large chair in the Inn's comfortable living room and there, to a pleasant sound of diminishing rain, he sipped a cordial, smoked and, under the drooping lids of weariness, continued the inexhaustible reverie of lovers.

Chapter 13

On the afternoon of storm, so congenial to the mood of Robin Ashe, Sally came out into the unthreatened sunshine of four o'clock to the stables ready for her duty of equestrian instruction. She was depressed. Joseph Marr that morning had advised strongly against her idea of breaking free from the peonage of Crewe House.

"I might," he had told her, "with your mother's consent, arrange for a small loan, though what security you could offer, my dear Miss Sally, is problematical, to say the least. But on my visit to your mother only yesterday, while you were out on horseback, I believe, she expressed herself as satisfied with her situation. To tell you the truth, I have never seen your mother more cheerful and at ease. She is happy to have you with her, to be taken care of by you. She has—and let us be thankful for it, Miss Sally!—taken a real liking to this Mr. Obadiah Crewe. It would be against her wish, I am sure, for you to borrow on a doubtful future and to go out to work in order to support yourself and an expensive invalid. It would be most unlikely, I should think, with all the will and talent in the world, that you should be able to earn anything like the sum of $3600 per annum, in addition to living expenses for two. No, my dear," he patted her shoulder, "I advise you to accept your situation with what cheerfulness and patience you can muster and see what the future may bring for its alleviation."

"So that," Sally now thought, slapping her slim boot with her riding cane and scowling with the ferocious schoolboy energy of which her mobile face was capable, "is *that*." She set her teeth upon it. "This devil has got around Mother and Marr. I'll have to wait for him to do something obviously outrageous before I get any break at all. There is this," she thought wickedly, "I *could* provoke him to something. He has a vile temper and an evil tongue. If I could make him good and *mad*." So Sally, musing and looking like a blonde Medea, came stablewards.

The door to the harness room was open and from it, as she approached, there came a sound of splashing and Jock's voice.

". . . not my business?" he was growling painfully. "Of course it's my business. It's the business of any decent man that knows her, Dad. That's what it is. She's thoroughbred and I'm for her, I tell you. I'll fight for her all up and down the country. 'Got it straight from someone in the house . . . a bunch of sightseers overheard him . . .' That's what the bloody liar said. I wager the bunch got it from that yellow old tomcat, Monkey. Mrs. Winter did her darnedest to get rid of him five years ago. Who else but me has she got to fight for her? Tell me that, Dad."

Sally's step was audible. The tirade stopped. She whistled and called, "Ready, Jock?" and in an instant he emerged. One eye was closed and there was a swollen cut at the corner of his mouth.

"Sorry to look like such a mess," grinned Jock carefully, and for the first time in her acquaintance with him, avoiding her eye. "I got into a fight in Hanbury this morning. Dad's been going over me for it. I'm a sight sure enough but then you don't have to ride with me anyhow."

Sally said slowly, "You must not fight for foolish reasons, Jock," her troubled gaze upon him.

Color smote his face. "You heard something, Miss Sally?"

"I couldn't help hearing part of what you said. You've been fighting for some girl and, of course, being a girl myself, I can't help liking you for it but I do hate to see you all battered up. Somehow, what idiots say is not worth that, quite, is it?"

"It's worth more than a black eye to me," he muttered and turned with his shoulders up and his head down to lead out Plucky to Vincent Crewe who, unobserved by Sally, had come meanwhile into the yard.

Vincent grinned down at Jock's injuries but said nothing about them until he and Sally were outside the stable gates.

"Where did he pick up the grand one? What was the kid grousing about to you?"

"He wasn't grousing. He'd got into a fight. Someone in the village said something about his girl. Who would it be, Mr. Crewe? It was someone in the house, I gathered from what he said. But there are no white girls."

"Brunn, the gardener, has a pretty daughter."

Sally's face cleared. "Of course. That's who it was. Nancy Brunn. Only I heard him say, 'She's got no one else to fight for her.'"

Vincent turned in his saddle carefully and set his eyes upon her.

"You got an earful, didn't you, Miss Keyne?"

"He was shouting and the door was wide open. I tried to whistle so that he could hear me but he was fairly orating. Mr. Crewe," she asked abruptly, "do you like Sebastian Manchi?"

"What brings him in?"

"Well, I think it was some gossip he had spread about the girl; talking about her to one of the tourists, or something, that provoked Jock's fight."

"That so? No. I don't like him."

"Then why do you keep him on?"

"Because, like several other members of my household, he was wished on to me in Uncle Caleb Winter's will."

Her face flamed.

"You dare," she cried between her teeth, looking at him with all her blazing eyes, "you dare to taunt my mother and me . . ."

"Steady! I can't afford to ride with a lady in a rage. Plucky's about all I can handle. I wasn't thinking of you. Yes, I was. But I only said it to make your eyes flare up. They are the darnedest eyes, they change color like a South American chameleon. You've got a regular old-fashioned temper, haven't you, Miss Sally?"

She was silent, her eyes cold and her color gone.

"You still sit your horse too rigidly," she said fifteen minutes later. "That's one reason you get so stiff."

"How do you know I get stiff?"

"The way you walk and stand and sit. Besides, if you get thrown, with all your muscles tight, you'll be hurt. The way to fall," said Sally, "is just to relax all over, fold your arms loosely over your chest, drop your head forward and roll free."

"You reckon I'll be able to strike that pose in an emergency?"

"It would be good for you to take a fall or two," said Sally sternly. "It would sort of loosen you up. They say it takes seven falls to make a rider."

Vincent drawled, "Well maybe I can take the first of the seven this afternoon. There's a big black storm coming up behind us and Plucky, I bet my head, don't like thunder one bit."

"That reminds me," said Sally, "you ought to wear a hat. It would save you if you ran against a branch."

"Sunshine on the scalp," he replied, grinning. "I'm letting my hair grow. Monkey's instructions. It's got me all balled up, this being a gentleman."

Sally, against her will, looked at his head. The hair was growing in and she saw that it was of the right Crewe color, a dark auburn, darker with him, in the new growth where it had not been bleached by a tramp's exposure.

"Will you wear sideburns?"

"Had I ought to?"

"They'd be rather becoming. You'd look eighteenth century English."

"Anything to please you and Monkey!"

From that he went on unexpectedly, although the connection in thought was obvious enough, "Which counts most, history or poetry?"

"How do you mean, counts most?"

"In the education of a gentleman?"

Sally considered. "History nowadays, I think. Men don't quote poetry nor 'read it out.' . . . It's not, for some reason, the thing."

He looked blank. "I get you. But I reckon I like poetry. Did you ever read a piece called 'Lady Claire' by Tennyson?"

"Yes. I did read it ... ages ago."

> " 'It was the time when lilies blow
>   And clouds are highest up in air
>   Lord Ronald brought a lily white doe
>   To give to his cousin, Lady Claire ...'

It turns out that she isn't by rights the lady and that he had ought to own the property.

> " 'He laughed a laugh of merry scorn,
>   He turned and kissed her where she stood.
>   If you are not a lady born
>   And I, said he, the next in blood ...

> " 'If you are but a beggar born
>   And I, said he, the rightful heir,
>   We two shall wed tomorrow morn
>   And you shall still be Lady Claire.' "

"Why do you learn by heart such silly dated stuff as that?"

He reddened a little but said surlily, "I like it. Anyhow, there's a heap of history books in the library. Do I begin with the ancient countries and work up or with 'Our Own Times' and work back?"

"I should say, take your choice. Except that past history sort of explains the present."

"I reckon, though, that I'll begin with now," he said. "It seems to me ..." then interrupted himself sharply and she saw a look of white concern fit itself close upon his face. "Why did you look so at that clump of trees?"

"Did I? Well, it's because on my first ride with Jock my horse was frightened just here by a tramp."

"Tramp?"

"Don't tighten up on Plucky like that. It makes him nervous." She remembered the night when Vincent had put out all the lights and prowled forth with a gun in his pocket. "You are timid about trespassers, aren't you? I think the tramp that scared Star was the same horrible man that got past Charles into the house. You saw him, didn't you?"

Vincent relaxed in body and expression. "You won't see him again."

"I should hope not. What did he want?"

"What everyone wants of me now . . . money."

"You gave him some?"

"Sure I did. Why did he bother you?"

"He frightened me."

"Why?"

"He was a dreadful-looking creature and he stared at me when I went through the hall."

"Judas!" ejaculated Vincent. "Crowded again! You had ought to wear a veil."

Sally was scarlet.

"One doesn't expect to be stared at by hoboes in one's own home."

Vincent grinned horridly. "Doesn't one? He wasn't a hobo and it ain't your own home."

Silence. Sally loped and that imprisoned her pupil's full attention.

Slowing for a descent, "Look here," said Vincent, "speaking of home and hoboes, I'm getting a pile of mail from folks nowadays and about three-quarters of it I don't know rightly how to answer. Can you earn your bread and butter by doing some social secretary work for me, mornings? This keeping house for one lone tramp don't seem to take you more'n half an hour and I'm paying you three hundred bucks per month."

"I will take care of your mail."

"Good. And, look a here, some of these classy folks about here have begun to leave their cards and I've been queried about belonging to the hunt and joining the country club and charities and a hospital and what not."

"You would be, of course."

"And I've got an invitation from a Mrs. Ernest Vintry . . ."

Sally said, "Oh!" and gave him a queer, quick look.

"Also, a Reverend's called upon me."

"Yes?"

"Well, will you serve tea or drinks for me around calling time if I get caught?"

Sally hesitated. "I wonder," she said and it was the first time this had occurred to her, "if people will understand."

"Understand what?"

"My position in the house. I don't think anyone knows about Mother's first marriage or ... or me ... at all."

"Old Mr. Marr knows."

"Yes. But I doubt if he goes around much or talks about people ever."

"Well, the best cure for not knowing about you is for folks to get to see you. You can tell them who you are and all that."

"Yes ... I suppose I can."

They rode in silence, blue sky ahead, the clouds rolling up unheeded in back of them.

Vincent broke out. "It's rot," he cried, "a will like that of old Winter's. Let's forget it and live like we were meant to. That house is big enough for an army and has help enough for a regiment of staff officers. What you say? Let's forget the lousy thing. I'm your mother's nephew sort of, and you and I can kind of play like we're cousins. What you say? How about it?"

Sally was instantly aware of danger. Of a motive in ambush. His eyes, their lids drawn narrow, were the eyes of a poker player. The watchdog in her subconscious stirred and growled. She gave him a long, cold and wary look.

"Thank you very much, Mr. Crewe. It's kind of you but I think we'd better accept the situation for what it is—awkward but not to be helped—and try to make the best of it."

He had pulled his horse so close that his boot touched her stirrup and was staring at her with an intentness which, having no expression to soften or to enliven it, made his narrow slate eyes look almost blind. She bore the look, keeping her own eyes steady and her face proud.

He looked down and shrugged the shoulders that were too broad and heavy for his hawk's head.

"O.K. If you want it to be like that." He muttered a few more words, something that sounded like "the old lady would likely have more sense."

Both horses jumped sidelong at a thunder shot.

Vincent reined in hard.

"Better go back."

"The storm's behind us. There's an Inn about three miles from here ... closer now than Crewe House. I think we're not more than a mile from the highway and the Inn would be the nearest place to try for."

"All right. Make it snappy."

She touched her mare with the light riding cane and both made rapid progress down their leafy lane.

But faster than horses' hooves came the flying feet of storm. Before they came out on the highroad they were caught. Rain flogged them, lightning sent Star and Plucky dancing and a thunderclap gave to the latter's self-possession its coup de grace. He took his bit in his teeth and ran.

The lane followed the usual pleasant vagaries of country lanes and, even without the veil of falling water, Sally would almost instantly have lost sight of her pupil. She was in terror for him: that intense and fundamental sympathy of one human creature for his endangered fellow, at once submerging the individual, personal hate. She suffered fantastic visions of a young man's death, saw Vincent dragged, kicked, mutilated, saw him in a thousand crushed and crippled ways so that, when she did actually come upon him flung down against the roadside with his head and shoulders in a ditch it was almost a relief so much less dreadful seemed the reality than the least of her imaginings. Plucky had vanished into the streaming, windy world.

Sally tied her own restive mount to the nearest fence rail and hurried to examine Vincent. She was instantly on her knees beside him, pulling away the wet weeds and grasses from his face. He had struck his head against a stone, was bleeding and unconscious. His color was that of death but she could feel his heart beat and hear the slow irregular breath. The rain emptied its reservoirs upon them, both drenched now to the skin.

Sally moved Vincent with sobbing difficulty so that his head was slightly higher than his heels and spread out uselessly over him her coat, as wet as his. Then, getting up to Star's slippery saddle, she sent the mare off in the direction of Grassways Inn. There she could get help, shelter, telephone for a doctor, get word to the house of her whereabouts, of Plucky's getaway, her own safety and Crewe's accident.

It was a blind, slithering, leaping ride and she could never quite remember how she got Star past the Inn's gateposts, glittering under their lights, but, once beyond these dragons, Star decided that nothing else could matter now and stood meekly in the porte-cochere, allowing her to dismount. She stood for a moment, stunned by the stillness, the cessation of wind and rain. Then she opened the Inn door and advanced into the big well-lighted entrance hall. A clerk at the desk rose with a cry of consternation.

"You were caught in the storm!"

"Yes ... but ..."

"On horseback, miss?"

"Yes. And will you please get someone to take my mare? She's outside in the porte-cochere. But, wait a moment! The man I was riding with has been thrown and hurt. We must go out and bring him in here at once."

In a mirror she caught a glimpse of herself, hatless; her hair sleeked down her face, every bit of her clothing plastered to her body, her boots slopping water.

"Let me get Mr. Grange, the manager. They're all at dinner. You want to telephone?"

"For a doctor ... and to tell my mother that I'm safe."

By the time she had accomplished these two urgent intentions, the Inn had got its station wagon to the door and Sally, refusing to change into dry clothes, climbed, dripping, into it with the manager and two other men.

"It's Mr. Crewe," she told them.

"Obadiah Crewe ... the new owner of Winter's place?"

Her affirmation seemed to increase their sense of his importance. They drove as fast as wind and rain allowed but, when they reached the lane, crept close to its side, following Sally's anxious search with all their eyes. She cried out first, "There he is," and in an instant they were all out, bending over the still unconscious man.

"Looks to me like a fracture or a concussion," said Grange. "Hope Dr. Minor will be at the Inn by the time we get Crewe back. It's a ticklish business to move a man with a fractured skull. You must drive slow, Jackson, and keep clear of the bumps ... if you can see them through this downpour."

They lifted Crewe into the car and laid him on its floor between the two lengthwise station wagon seats, where Sally too crouched down, holding his head on her knees between her hands to steady it. The light in the ceiling of the car shone down on the wet, pallid, evenly set features, making of them a mask with the curious beauty and terror of a mask. That face, she thought, can't possibly ever live again and, dead, the man called Vincent did not seem the same being. This still face was the face of a stranger and, as such, was mysterious, noble, something that might have been beloved. It had sweetness. The heavy lips were gentle in their quiet lines. The closed lids, lashed in dark red, were childlike, pitiable.

When they reached the Inn Dr. Minor had not yet arrived. There had been difficulty in locating him, the clerk said. "They'd get him, though, he'd surely be on his way before long." Vincent was carried into one of the bedrooms and there his wet clothing was cut or carefully drawn away and he was covered in blankets. Sally, also in borrowed garments, topped by a flannel wrapper, sat, slippered, beside him, watching for signs of returning consciousness. She had put a hot water bottle at his feet, a wet pad underneath the wound in his head. It lay in the exact middle of the pillow, no stone effigy more carved and colorless. But his eyes now seemed to be only partly closed, a fact which increased the look of recent death. His hands were covered. There was of her enemy only this detached, inanimate head. After about an hour, his eyes opened and Vincent spoke.

"Look here, don't you let him come in without giving me a chance to talk to him, will you, darling?" he said softly.

Sally looked about her for help, then chided her own cowardice. He was pulling out one of his white naked arms, stretching towards her its dark red hand. She tried to cover the arm and shoulder but he had them out again at once.

"If Fred gets in before I tell him about how it happened, it will be a mighty tough break for me. It's not so much getting killed I mind but it's him killing me . . . old Fred . . . and never knowing why I did it. See? When did you get back, Tinka? I thought it was a sure thing that you were dead."

Sally said the usual, "Hush. It's all right," soothingly. "I won't let anyone come in."

"If you aren't dead sure enough, you know, it's a queer mess. But I got the evidence. Only . . . about Fred . . . look here, you promise you won't let him get in. He was just outside the window while you were playing on the piano."

"Of course I promise." Sally felt a chilly puckering of her skin. "He doesn't know you're here."

"You'll recognize him, won't you, Sally, if he comes to leave his card?"

That startled her. "Vincent!" She bent down closer. "You're coming to yourself, aren't you? You do know me?"

"Sure I know you, you little stiff-necked devil, and I'll break you good and plenty before I'm through. It's room you want, is it? I'll teach you the meaning of close quarters . . . sure. But you'll know him, anyway. Fred's got a narrow face, like a knife, see? Black eyes, kind of close together, a long nose. He's got a grand build. Like a gentleman, not too heavy, see? He talks mighty low; you got to listen close to hear him."

"Oh, please try to lie quiet. Keep your head still, Vincent!"

"Did Fred shoot me?"

"No. You were thrown from your horse. Plucky was frightened by the thunder storm and ran."

"Sure. I remember. Fred came out from behind one of those buttonwood trees and let me have it. Got me back of the ear like he said he would. Why didn't you give me a chance to tell him?" He stopped, looked searchingly up at her with changed young eyes, widely opened. "Sally . . . Sally . . . Sally . . ."

She wished he would not repeat her name. She would gladly have put her hand across his mouth. Such a curious variety of tones: reproach, tenderness, longing, anger and suspicion, a most moving, a most distressing gamut like the tale told by the idiot, "full of sound and fury and signifying nothing." But his voice was astonishingly beautiful and resonant. He should have been an actor. He could do anything with that voice. Now, in delirium, his face and mouth and eyes were all alive, like his voice, and changeful. The whole creature seemed afire with furious, uncurbed emotions. This was not the man she had known. The difference lay in two circumstances: the lack of rigid control and the enormous opening of his eyes. They made the rest of his face seem more slender, less important, not nearly so massive. They were young, brilliant eyes, sparkling blue grey, polished like crystals. Nothing of the poker player's changelessness about them.

"Hush, Vincent, hush." She put her hand upon his and instantly he lay still and was silent and looked at her. He smiled very slowly and simply and closed his lids. So she kept her gentle and warm grasp on his fingers which twitched and fidgeted, although he seemed to be asleep.

After about another hour, "I'm thirsty," he said. "Got some water, Sally?"

There had been some but she had drunk it herself. She drew away her hand and went to the bell button beside the door. She saw Vincent was trying to sit up and hurried back.

"Lie down. If you will promise me to lie perfectly still, I'll go out and get you some ice water to drink right away."

"O.K." He lay down obediently.

She went out into the hall. There was no sign of any answering bellboy. The Inn was entirely silent and only the night lights burned. The long empty passage with its narrow crimson carpet made her think of the St. Charles Hotel and Room 825. Her longing for Robin made her stand still and close her eyes. She was about to go on, holding her borrowed wrapper close about her, towards a water filter she remembered seeing at the turn close to the head of the stairs, when she heard Vincent's voice calling in a muffled and frightened tone, "Sally . . . Sally . . . Sally . . ."

She returned to his door and opened it. He was looking anxiously for her but had not lifted his head.

"Don't call me, Vincent. I'll be right back . . . hush!"

She faced the hall again, softly shutting herself out,
and found that another visitor to the Inn had come out
of his room a few feet further up the hall and was
standing still to look at her. He was a tall man in a
grey travelling suit and his head was dark, curly and
narrow. She saw this and then she recognized him. It
was Robin Ashe.

He had, of course, seen her and was staring at her
fixedly. But when she gave a low exclamation and
made a quick step towards him, her lips open for
speech, he jerked his body back and away and strode as
rapidly as a man can without actually running from her
down the interminable passage and out of Sally's sight.
She called "Robin!" faintly and then a trifle louder. A
bellboy came up quickly behind her, just as she was
about to run after the longed-for apparition.

"Did you ring, ma'am?"

"Y . . . yes. We . . . want some ice water, please. Mr.
Crewe is conscious. He's thirsty and . . . and delirious, I
think."

"I guess you'll be glad to know that the doctor's just
come in, Mrs. Crewe. He's on his way up now."

Sally went in. Vincent seemed to have fallen asleep
again or perhaps into a coma. She stood staring at a
ghostly image of herself in the long mirror of the
bathroom door. Of course Robin hadn't recognized her.
She looked like "nothing human." Her hair was still
dark with rain and plastered down, her eyes were
shrunk within swollen lids, there was no color in her
face or mouth. And the shapeless wrapper made her
look like a long cylindrical mummy, straight from neck
to heel. He had simply wished to relieve a strange
woman in an unbecoming negligee of his embarrassing
presence. Why he was there at Grassways Inn was certainly something to wonder about, but not his lack of
recognition nor his swift wordless escape. When she got
back to Crewe House there would be news. Her blood
began to move to the drums of reassurance and delight.
This was the answer to her letter . . . Robin himself!

Here the doctor came in and she saw his eyes widen

upon her for an instant before he turned them quickly to his patient. She fancied that he thought her a wild figure. She did not guess that he thought her beautiful; desperate and tragic, the rumored condition of her life. Neither did she guess that Robin had left the Inn, thrown himself into his roadster and was flying through the still clear night with such pain of jealousy and shame, of tortured love and pride fastened upon his sensitive spirit, as he had never before imagined that a man might be called upon to endure.

Chapter 14

Vincent Crewe was suffering from a concussion, not too serious, but had better, the doctor said, not be moved from his bedroom at Grassways Inn. A nurse was sent for and Sally before noon of the bright warm day that followed upon the storm, mounted Star and rode home where, at the stables, she found that Jock had retrieved Plucky none the worse for his fright. As soon as she had visited her mother and given an account of yesterday's misadventure, Sally hurried to her own room and eagerly took up the little pile of her mail. It contained the expected telegram from Robin Ashe.

"Letter received. Rescue all lined up. On my way to put plan over with your help. Will see family first. You on Thursday. Love."

Today, the calendar told Sally, widening her eyes upon it, was Friday. She rushed downstairs, summoned Charles, Henry, Early, everyone. There was no evidence of any ardent visitor to see Miss Sally—no young gentleman at all. Unless the entire staff of Crewe House had played truant or slept at its post, Robin Ashe had not put in his promised appearance. Yet she had seen him with her own eyes at Grassways Inn and Grassways Inn was close to Hanbury.

Perhaps he had quarrelled with his family, perhaps they had on her account turned him out. But wouldn't he then have come straight to her? Flushing, paling, changing her dress, rearranging her hair, putting on lipstick and rubbing it off, wandering, listening, looking, starting, Sally, at last, after three terrible days, was driven by the misery of the suspense past pride to that magic maker for divided criminals and lovers, the telephone.

She shut fast the office door and with shaking fingers turned the leaves of the telephone book to the name of Ronald Ashe at Fallows. She moved the dial jerkily, sat pale and empty of expression until her color flashed up at the sound of an answering voice.

"Hullo."

"Hullo. Is this the home of Mr. Ronald Ashe?"

"Yes, madam."

"May I . . . I wonder if I . . . can speak to Mr. Robin Ashe?"

"Mr. Robin is not at home now, madam."

"Not at home? But he's staying somewhere in the neighborhood, isn't he?"

"I'm not sure, madam. You might try at his sister's, Mrs. Ernest Vintry's."

"Oh, thank you. Yes."

She hung up and began again, this time with tears on her eyelashes, to look down the listed names. Vintry. Ernest Vintry. Hanbury 208.

Another voice, a particularly clear and high-pitched one, no servant's certainly.

"Hullo."

"Hullo. I wonder if I might speak to Mr. Robin Ashe."

"Who is this, please?"

"Sally Keyne, at Crewe House. I want to speak to Mr. Robin Ashe."

"Just a moment, please." Whoever it was left the telephone and Sally could hear a step across the floor and the closing of a door. Returned, the speaker said, "Miss Keyne, this is Robin's sister, Hazel Vintry."

"Oh, yes, Mrs. Vintry. Is Robin with you?"

"Not now. He was for two nights and a day last week. He has gone back to New Haven."

"I . . . I have a wire from him. He expected to . . . to see me . . ."

"I dare say." Hazel Vintry paused then began, in a more determined voice, to speak again. "Miss Keyne, I believe the best plan would be for me to read aloud to you over the telephone a letter Robin left for me when he returned to college. Can you hear me?"

"Oh yes. Perfectly." If only, she thought, my heart would stop this racketing!

"You are alone?"

"Yes. Yes, I am. Entirely."

"Very well. Just a second. I'm at my desk and the letter is under my hand. Ready? This is the letter Robin left for me when he went back to Yale. 'Dear Hazel . . .' You are sure you can hear me?"

"Oh, yes, Mrs. Vintry."

"Dear Hazel: Do put me right with Dad and Mother. They were of course absolutely correct and I was a fool. I've gone back to Yale to fix up the exam matter. I think I can wrangle a new deal. Hazel . . . I saw her with that man. They were together in a room at Grassways Inn. It was past midnight. She came out into the hall. So what the guide told you and Mother is true, she is his 'housekeeper by courtesy.' I might have known after the way she picked me up at the hotel in Baltimore. But I never met anyone who did it better. I'm almost out of my head with shame; it will take me a long time to get over it . . . and to get over her. You never really saw her, Hazel. She is wonderful. The most wonderful girl I ever knew. Excuse this crossword puzzle. I don't know what I'm writing. I never was so nearly crazy in my life. Or so sick. You know, I always thought a broken heart was a kind of figure of speech. It isn't. Robin."

The wires hummed and hummed in Sally's ears.

"Miss Keyne, are you still there?"

"Yes, Mrs. Vintry. Thank you. I understand now. I . . . I didn't know the world could be so horribly wrong, and so cruel to anyone. Good-bye."

She hung up blindly, uncertainly, and her bright, tawny head came forward slowly and slowly down until it rested on the top of the desk. One of her hands was clenched upon an open page of verse . . .

> *"With thy clear keen joyaunce,*
> *Languor cannot be,*
> *Shadow of annoyance*
> *Never came near thee . . ."*

The languor of grief did not at once overcome Sally's natural keenness. At first pride and anger proved anæsthetic and she was able to appear before her mother and the household with laughter, color and bright eyes. But the nights with their stillness and their stars and their winds of midsummer weakened her resentment, brought the anguish of disappointed hope and thwarted yearning. She had not realized how absolutely she had counted upon Robin's heroic rescue.

So, at last, being no Victorian miss, she wrote a letter.

"Dear Robin: If someone had told me a dreadful story against you, proving you a liar or a rotter and a cad, even if I'd seen you in some compromising position, that seemed like absolute evidence against you, I'd have remembered your face and voice and eyes . . ." Here her tears poured on the paper and she had to make a fresh start. "I'd have remembered your face and voice and eyes and I'd have said, 'I know him better than that.' I think I'd have stood up for you against the world, Robin. I even think if you had really done something wrong I'd have counted over the difficulty and the temptation that had made it possible for you. But there's no use telling what I'd have done when I know now what you have done. You did, I think, from what I got between the lines of that letter your sister read out to me over the telephone . . . (and I want you please, Robin, to read her this letter . . . or at least the part that explains) I think you did refuse to believe the malicious gossip of a mulatto servant and I do thank you for that much trust. But when you saw me at the Inn that night . . . (I thought you didn't recognize me because I looked such a fright) saw me come out of Mr. Crewe's room and speak to him by his name, then you did believe and you didn't even give me a chance to explain or to defend myself.

"I suppose if I was very, very proud I'd just let you think what you please and let you go without trying to change your opinion of me, but I'm not as proud as that. I think I was beginning to love you terribly . . ."

Here again she had to lean back to save her page from tears.

"Now, I don't want to see you again. I don't want to

think of you. After I've closed this letter, I am going to forget you. I've plenty of will power and I can do anything I make up my mind to do. I am not going to let any man ... no, nor any woman or child" ... unconsciously she quoted Miss Culpepper ... "ruin my life. But I do want you to understand your mistake."

She then briefly set down the story of her ride, the accident, the truth of her predicament at Grassways Inn.

"I know that I was a fool to stay here at Crewe House as housekeeper. But you must understand how that came about. Mother doesn't think of the sort of thing people are saying because she's sick and out of the world and because she trusts Vincent Crewe more than I can (he has talked her around somehow) and because, I guess, she doesn't realize that I didn't figure at all in any of the newspaper accounts of Mr. Winter's will, so that very few people realize I am her daughter.

"Mr. Marr knows but I think his theory is that the less said about Mother's first marriage and her keeping it and me a secret, the less talk there will be. I don't suppose this horrid explanation of me being here has ever entered into his kind mind of a gentleman. I know now that there has been a lot of talk. Jock Nunn, the stable boy, has fought about me in Hanbury ... he was more loyal than you, Robin! ... and I know that the story was started by a dreadful little Jamaican mulatto named Sebastian Manchi who has a grudge against my mother. I don't know what I shall do. Mother must not be troubled or distressed. A shock of this kind might be fatal to her. She must never hear a word of this. I don't know how I can make the truth known, or live down the rumor. Everyone believes it now, everyone wants to believe it. But I do know this ... I will never again trust a man that looks and smiles like you. Sally."

And then she had to leave the little writing table and fling herself down upon her bed, for his face and eyes and smile were vivid and endearing to her memory and the thought of never seeing or trusting them again twisted her heartstrings.

Mrs. Winter suspected nothing of her daughter's unhappiness nor did the servants appear to notice any difference in the gallant young presence to which they had grown accustomed; but no sooner had the master of the house returned, than Sally knew herself to be unmasked.

This undesired event occurred sooner than anyone would have believed possible. One week sufficed Vincent for what he considered a complete recovery. He had changed, lost the deep copper of his sunburn, and his hair, grown out quickly, made a close rust-colored border about his thinned face. To Sally's wan amusement he had actually encouraged sideburns, evidently convinced that they were part of the desired aspect of a Virginian gentleman. And they did bring out a remarkable resemblance between him and some of the Crewe portraits.

Sally had been eating her meals, or trying in a heartbroken fashion to eat them, at the small breakfast table in the downstairs dining room and she was at dinner there on the evening of Vincent's return.

She heard the sound of a motor, of opening doors and footsteps, looked around and there almost beside her, he stood. He wore a new suit of most correct and becoming cut and color ... for Manchi had returned from his mission to the New York tailor ... beautiful linen and a gay attractive tie. He was smartly shod and socked and an initialed handkerchief protruded from his coat pocket. Altogether, the change in his appearance was startling, but he had resumed his poker face and his eyes were close lidded, cold and grey. She could not help but remember the relationship in which she was supposed to stand to this man and felt the blood rush up painfully into her face as she rose to greet him.

"You are back ... all well ... so soon?"

"It don't seem like soon to me," he said with the old soft roughness; "it seems like tardy. Got some dinner for me?"

Charles, bobbing and smiling and wishing joy, pulled up a chair.

"Not the sort of dinner you like," said Sally, dreading the accomplished tête-à-tête . . . he had never seemed so close, so overpowering as seated opposite her, his knees not twelve inches from her own beneath the cloth. "No T-bone steak nor fried potatoes."

"O.K.," he said. "Now I am an invalid, the other

kind of food goes down all right. Anyhow I can't eat like I use to. Don't get enough hard exercise. I reckon, Miss Sally, you'd better go back to planning my meals. Likely," he grinned, "clear soup and chops in ruffled pants and soufflés and greens kind of shape down the figure like a gentleman's."

Charles had brought a cup of clear soup which Vincent now sipped gingerly.

Now and again he glanced up quickly at his vis-à-vis.

"Your mother making good progress?" he asked her in the voice of a cautious investigator and she realized that he had read her face and eyes, read that new strained look about her lips, and was bent upon discovering the reason for it. Her pride and reserve, her terror of his knowledge flashed up color and a look of cheerfulness into her face and she began to chatter as was her way when some emotion loosened her tongue. She told him household incidents that were funny ... she hadn't even smiled at them when they had occurred ... queer words and sayings of the blacks ... she made a history of nothing. Vincent listened. Except for the lack of expression he was a wonderful listener. His sign of amusement was a turning down and away of his head and a sort of throaty chuckle, a most contagious sound of mirth absolutely not, by all the force of his will to gravity, to be repressed. After dessert he said, "Fetch the coffee into the big parlor, will you, Charles? Miss Sally, I would like to hear some piano playing again."

She was almost as grateful for this suggestion as she would have been for an immediate escape.

In the living room when Charles had brought the silver coffee urn and tiny cups, setting them before Sally, erect in a formal Chippendale chair, Vincent spoke sharply.

"I see you've forgotten one of my orders, Charles."

The old butler rolled his eyes. "I'm certainly apoplectic, Mr. Crewe."

"He means 'apologetic,'" Sally murmured at Vincent's startled look.

"I certainly did forget. Mrs. Winter she always lak the windows wide for summer nights," and he went quickly about pulling to the shutters and drawing the curtains close.

It was a warm evening and the room seemed to Sally airless and oppressive.

"Not taking any coffee, Miss Sally?" Vincent asked as she poured his, then sat back and lighted herself a cigarette.

Sally shook her head, her soft hair swinging and shining under the light of a lamp behind her. She did not tell him that her nights were terrible enough without incitation to greater wakefulness.

"If you like," she said aloud, attempting her smile, "I can play for you now while you drink yours."

"O.K."

She hurried over and sat down before the keys. She played at random and by memory, improvising what she forgot, aimless and wistful music, familiar melodies.

He sat, his elbows on his knees, holding the tiny golden cup in his big hands and looking up at her; looking at her steadily, looking at her until she longed to cry out at him and put up her hands before her face. When he had finished his coffee, he rolled and lighted himself a cigarette and began his steady rhythmic pacing. But still he watched her . . . no merciful turning off of lights. At last, stopping by the piano and leaning close, "There's a tune you played that other night," he said.

She softened her chords and lifted her great eyes.

"A tune?"

"Yes. It's something I must have heard often. It's an old tune. Wait," he began to whistle,

"What's this dull town to me?
Robin's not here."

"I don't think I can play that."

"Why not? That's the way it goes. Listen again."

"Yes. That's the way it goes."

She opened her eyes to a shining and dazed width, her face paled, her lips still by long custom soft, drew close and sharpened their fine geranium edges. She gave her mane a quick little jerk and then she played.

"Aren't there any words? It's a song, isn't it?"

"Yes."

Without any change of face she sang, in a throaty boyish voice, sweet but uncertain of its strength.

> *"What's this dull town to me?*
> *Robin's not here.*
> *What was't I wished to see*
> *What wished to hear?*
> *Where's all the joy and mirth*
> *Made this place heaven on earth . . ."*

She had trusted her control too far. Sudden as tropic storm, came an acute realization of her loss, of her pain. It was as though she had made public confession, abandoned her pride and her reserve. Her voice broke, her eyes filled, her face quivered, she put up her hands and burst into a girl's passion of crying.

Vincent crushed out his cigarette, stood watching her an instant and then sprang to her side and took her closely into his arms.

"Don't you cry. Don't you cry."

It was to Sally as incredible an event as if a tree had stepped into the room and pressed its bark against her. Hard and warm his body was . . . the heart laboring under her ear. His hands, grasping her head, pressed her hair up in a sort of crest, awkward and urgent, wildly tender.

"Don't Sally. I can't bear it. You mustn't cry . . ." and he fairly drew her up from her bench, turned her face to his and kissed her mouth.

Sally broke from him at that and fled but he overtook her at the door.

"No!" she cried. "No! I can't bear it!" She choked and set her teeth together. "You hate me. I hate you. People think . . . people say . . ."

"What?" he asked her, keeping himself a foot away from her but still between her and her intended exit. "What do people say?"

"Can't you imagine?" she cried, crimson and shaking, glittering her wet eyes at him. "Nobody knows who I am. I came here almost when you came. Can't you imagine what they say? Maybe you want them to think that? Maybe you helped to start the story. Maybe that's the way you planned to punish me. I was proud and wanted too much room ... so you are going to crush my independence and—and bring me so close to you that ... that I won't have room to breathe. Oh, you know I'm absolutely helpless, that Mother mustn't be troubled or scared. Perhaps you meant ..."

"Shut up, you little fool," he said roughly and she stopped. "You know you're talking rot. I've been loving you ever since I looked up and saw you on the steps and you pulled your dress away from me. You know I've been loving you. You know it. I've seen it in your eyes. That boy of yours—the one that knocked me down—he's gone back on you because of this talk, hasn't he? I know his sort. A guy that knocks a man down just to show off to a woman—when he knows he's safe against any comeback. O.K. If they're talking about you and me and saying ugly things, let's fix it up and get married. Pronto. Your mother's for it. I've talked to her. Look a here, Sally ..." She was staring with her mouth open and as little expression in her face as a baby or a flower. "It'll be like ... that poem you told me was dated ...

> *"If you are but a beggar born*
> *And I, said he, the next in blood.*
> *If you are but a beggar born*
> *And I, said he, the rightful heir ...*
> *We two shall wed tomorrow morn*
> *And you shall still be Lady Claire."*

And then Sally, looking straight at him, began to laugh.

She laughed until her throat narrowed and her breath caught. "Oh, let me go, let me go!" she gasped and this time he did step to one side and opened the door for her escape. She fled up the stairs, holding to the banisters, laughing, crying, struggling for self-control. She did not know ... she never knew ... with what countenance Vincent stood and watched her flight.

Chapter 15

Sally had once been taken to an amusement park where there had been a hall of Laughing Mirrors, in which she had seen her world, her companions and herself turned topsy turvy and distorted to an extent that had excited—for she was very young—less of her risibility than of her fears. Now, having gradually overcome the hysteria of shock that had trod too closely on her pain, she lay on her narrow bed of a maid servant, her bare arm thrown childishly across her eyes, and envisaged a world completely asymmetrical. Her picture of life at Crewe House had been mirrored in her certainty of Vincent's hatred of her, his desire to punish her. Now, if she could believe his words, if they and the quaint quotation had not been mockery, she knew that he loved her, had, in the Victorian fashion, "spoken to her mother," had asked her in the most explicit terms, decorated by verses, also Victorian, to be his wife. What, in the name of wonder, then, thought Sally, had been the wisdom of her intuitional warnings . . . why had she so disliked and feared this man?

For the first time in days she was delivered from the misery of Robin Ashe by being obsessed by the mystery of Vincent Crewe. Gradually, as her laughter went to sobbing and her sobbing to sighing, and her sighing to slow even breaths, she began to see Vincent without the lurid aura of her interpretation of him. And the first thing her unprejudiced eye discerned was just his youth.

If I had met him out somewhere, at a friend's house, at some party, on a tennis court, I'd have thought him a shy, quaint, rough boy, who had in some fashion been forced into a harsh maturity of self-protection and of self-control. If he had had bad blood,

130

thought Sally now, he'd be like that little cur that followed him up from Hanbury, or vicious like the fierce
dog of a tramp. It's good blood that has made him
tough and it's gentle blood that has made him quaint, a
secret and serious love of beauty, of quiet learning and
quiet speech. She remembered belatedly the tone in
which he had said to her, "We two will wed tomorrow
morn, And you shall still be Lady Claire." A tone triumphant, touched with laughter, wistful. For he had
longed to say, I want to put you back where you belong. I want to make you amends for my artificial and
accidental supremacy. Like the child in the poem he
"hated to go above" her. He was offering the best he
had. He could not bear to see her cry, to watch her
pain and her humiliation. He would obliterate the
rumor and make her the Lady of Crewe House. Sally
sprang up. "I'll go down and beg his pardon," she told
her marred pale face, bathing it before the bathroom
mirror. "I'll go down and thank him for the honor he
has done me and I'll explain why I can't possibly marry
him . . . or ever anyone at all." And she looked away
from the glass not to see the returning quiver of her
lips.

Having restored the aspects of tranquillity, smoothed
down her rumpled yellow frock, a sleeveless school-girl
evening dress, she looked at her watch, found the night
still young . . . it was only half-past ten . . . and went
quickly along her passage to the central hall. At the
turn of the staircase she was stopped short by what she
saw under the hanging light of the great hall below.

The step where her astonished perception brought
her to a pause was, curiously, the same of that panic
which on the night of their first meal together, she had
suffered at the sight of Vincent waiting for her. It
seemed to Sally now that that past shrinking of her
nerves must have been simply a sort of second sight, a
warning of what she was now being forced to see. For
out of the door of the beautiful drawing room, shone
on by soft lights, looked down upon by the calm faces
of dead Crewes, supported on one side by Henry, the
tall gaunt young colored man, and on the other by
Vincent himself, came slowly a ghastly, ghostly, stutter-
ing, stooped figure, the figure of a blanched, rough

headed dirty old man—the tramp, in fact, who had startled Sally's horse and later scared herself by looking up at her in speculation from under his dingy falling lock of grey-blonde hair.

Vincent and Henry were now leading him along the hall. In another instant, Sally realized, they would be bringing him up the stairs on which she stood. This sent her up a few hasty steps and drew from her a small involuntary cry. Vincent then saw her. His face tightened.

"Don't bring that man in here. Don't bring that man upstairs," Sally said softly, but with a voice as expressive of loathing as her eyes.

Vincent left his share of the burden to Henry and, running quickly up, took Sally by the arm and turned her about.

"Go back to your room and stay there." He was urging her, compelling her to reascend, she yielding but looking at him as they went with bewildered alarm in possession of her face. At the top, "Vincent," she began. He checked her, standing on the step below her, lifting his eyes, using a queer slow smile.

"After all, Sally," he said, "I have the right to tell you to go back where you belong. I am the master of the house."

This truth overcame her, her lids fell, her whole young face lost its rigidity of will and pride, went blank, defeated and ashamed. She drew herself from his grasp, ducking down her head like a child who won't cry for its punishment and went with quick steps away from the stair head along the dimly lighted passage to her room. She knew the terrible old man was being led up the stairs. She knew that he would pass the night under Crewe's roof, and the knowledge gave her a sickness that even to herself seemed out of all proportion to its cause.

She locked her door and found herself trembling and cold. Her instinct was to go to her mother, creep close against her, hide her face. But that refuge was not only denied but changed to a responsibility. Whatever happened, Isabella Winter must not know what manner of guest Crewe Mansion's master entertained. Out of that suspected past of his were beginning to emerge the ugly shapes of its obligations, its fears and shames and crimes.

Vincent's blood had drooped out of his face as though through a sudden wound when he had lifted it to see Sally on the stairs.

When she went to sleep that night she dreamed quite terribly. She was groping down an endless hall until suddenly she had come against a mirror. To meet her there had appeared the terrible blanched shaken image of the tramp. The face bobbed and moved almost to touch her own, but when she looked back, there was no one behind her ... no one in the whole long passage now as bright as noon. So she discovered with that blind white fear of dreams that the mirror had held only a reflection of herself.

Mrs. Winter, at breakfast the next morning, noticed her daughter's pallor. "Aren't you well, dear? Didn't you sleep last night?"

Sally moved from beside the bed, crossed the room to its open window and stood there looking down and away across the green fields from which a July sun had not yet sucked the freshness of their morning dew. To her mother was visible the straight and limber back, arms linked behind by two tightened hands, hair falling as though the chin were lifted high.

"Oh, well," said Sally, wheeling suddenly about with resolution opening her eyes and straightening her lips, "I had a" ... she substituted "surprise" for "shock" ... "last night."

"Not a pleasant one if it's made you so pale."

Sally gave a short laugh. "Vincent Crewe asked me to marry him."

She watched Mrs. Winter's face and saw, with a drop of her heart, that it brightened and flushed almost to the tint of health. She came over and caught at her mother's hand.

"You don't want me to marry him? You can't want that?"

"Why not, Sally?"

"Oh, Mother, Mother! That man? He ... he isn't like any of the boys I know, my friends, the brothers of my friends."

"Sally, he is a gentleman."

"In the deepest sense, perhaps he is. But he hasn't lived the sort of life I understand. He's had experiences, has done and been things, has known people that make him different. Mother," here she let fall her head and laid her cheek against the strong square palm, "I don't know what queer men and women would come climbing up at us out of his past. He ... scares me, Mother. There are a lot of secrets in his life. You can see them being kept out of sight, if you look into his face and eyes."

Mrs. Winter could not lift her free hand to lay it on Sally's head though she tried to do so. She said with grimness:

"There were quite a lot of secrets in my life, Sally. And you were one of them."

"A queer person enough, Mother?"

"A darling person. Perhaps Vincent hasn't so many dreadful secrets, Sally. Why don't you ask him?"

"But, Mother, it isn't only that. I don't love him."

"You don't know him. You've only just begun to know him. Can't you give him time? You don't love anyone else."

"No!" A muffled syllable but to Mrs. Winter's ears it had the sound of truth.

"Don't you see how perfect it would be for all of us, Sally?"

Sally sat up and began to laugh. Presently with the uneven voice of her ironic mirth she quoted ...

> *"O, and proudly up she stood.*
> *Her heart within her did not fail.*
> *She looked into Lord Ronald's eyes*
> *And told him all her nurse's tale ..."*

"Mother, do you remember the story of Lady Claire? No? Wait ... there's a Tennyson somewhere. I'm going to read it to you."

She actually went away, returned to the astonished invalid and read the poem from its first lines

> *"It was the time when lilies blow*
> *And clouds are highest up in air*

Lord Ronald brought a lily white doe
To give his cousin, Lady Claire . . ."

to its last: "We two will wed tomorrow morn, and you shall still be Lady Claire."

"That's what he quoted to me. You see, Mother, when we first met he was a 'beggar born' and I was a great lady." She told Mrs. Winter for the first time her story of the insolent hobo whom Robin had knocked down and whom she had put out of her car. "Now, he's pleased to condescend to the nurse's child."

"Sally, don't be so childish!"

"It was Vincent who was childish, Mother."

"But what on earth," cried Isabella the practical, "has that silly old sentimental stuff got to do with anything?"

"I don't know, dear." Sally laid aside the volume sadly and with weariness. "I don't know indeed. But it was my first offer of marriage. The boys nowadays sort of do things differently."

"And you weren't touched by this boy's way?"

"I was . . . a little."

"But you aren't now, on sober second thought?"

"On sober second thought, Mother darling, I think I'd rather die than marry Obadiah Vincent Crewe."

The square dark face lost its new color and in it were more apparent instantly the slight distortion and drooping of the muscles, lid and cheek and mouth. Sally looked away.

"And you are going to tell him that?"

"I must tell him that, Mother."

"Then what," and her mother's voice had changed and weakened, "what will become of us?"

For the first time Sally envisaged the possibility of catastrophe.

"You don't think he'll take it out on me . . . on you?"

"It might be more than he could bear, to have you in his house."

Sally sat, staring. "Then," she said, "I'll have to go."

Mrs. Winter pulled herself along her pillows and grabbed her daughter's arm in her well hand.

"I couldn't bear that. I didn't have you for so many years. Besides, I'm not well enough to . . . to keep the terms of Caleb's will. What would become of me?" Her voice broke suddenly to the terrible weak treble of old age.

"But, Mother, he can't be such a cad. He wouldn't turn you out."

"I can't stay here by his charity. And I'm not sure I could make this house my home legally, even if he asked me to. I don't know how binding in detail a will like Caleb's is."

"Oh!" cried Sally, "*he* was the beast . . . the brute."

Mrs. Winter said, "Hush," then added in a low voice, controlled to her usual tone and moving back to her pillow, "I deserved it. I lied to him about . . . Jack Keyne . . . and about you."

Sally sat then, her chin on her hand, her elbow on her knee, frowning and brooding.

"Well," she spoke in the hard sharp tone of frightened youth, "well, Mother, what are we to do? I'm not going to be one of these sacrifices on the altar of matrimony. There's a lot of things I'd rather be than that."

"I never asked you to sacrifice yourself."

"Don't worry, pet." Sally rose and smiled one of her biggest and most careless smiles. "I'll work it out somehow. I'll mitigate the tyrant's rage. I guess I can make him see sense."

"Sally, why not give him just a little . . . hope?"

Sally, looking down with a certain starry coldness at her mother, answered, "I haven't enough to spare, Mother. I'll do better. I'll give him a complete despair. And I'll try out his . . . makings of a gentleman."

"You frighten me!"

"I needn't. I believe I have more faith than you have in Vincent. I think he'd rather be cut up into little bits of pieces before me than not play the rôle of a Virginian cavalier. The young man has the pride of Prince Rupert. He might bow himself out of this house but he'll never have the courage to bow me out . . . and that goes for you too, Mother."

"Sally, I don't want you to be bitter and cruel. I don't want you to feel humiliated or at the mercy of anyone."

"Mother, my sweet, I'd rather by a whole lot be cruel and bitter than soft and secret and slavish. And I don't believe you can be humiliated or at the mercy of anyone if you just don't choose to be. Cheer up. I'll come out of this mess all right and get you out too. It's a big world. You're getting better every day. I've got some friends." She kissed her mother almost violently. "Just talking about it to you has cleared my mind. I feel as if I was made out of nice shiny limber steel. Good-bye. I'm going down to talk to Mr. Crewe."

But at the door she turned her keen, quick-colored countenance. "Just one question, Mother ... did you make Vincent any promise about ... about me?"

"Sally darling ..."

"Well, did you?"

"Of course not. I told him I'd be glad."

"And you'd still be glad to have me marry him if he were just a hobo, and not the 'rightful heir'?"

Mrs. Winter smiled up one side of her mouth and said nothing.

"But you do really like the boy?" asked Sally.

"I do indeed. I can certainly say that."

"For what reasons ... besides his being Lord Ronald?"

"Because he is honest and humble and gentle and brave."

"'Oh my Heavens!" cried Sally and went out, closing the door as carefully as though she had been, indeed, a Victorian maiden.

Chapter 16

She went down to her writing room with the motions of the springy steel she had described, shut its door and, leaning back, remembered how upon first entering she had liked this room, allowed its shadowed and sober seclusion to possess her. Like every other pleasant aspect of the house this sanctuary had been spoiled by its changed ownership. And there, with a great start, she saw that the owner was, standing in one of the deep window niches and looking at her with no expression on his face.

"I didn't see you," said Sally, angry for her own start, hating to be seen with the unmasked face of solitude. "You oughtn't to hide like that."

"I wasn't hiding." He came forward and as she went to her seat at the desk, stood in the middle of the floor with an air as though he were unconscious of all outer circumstance except herself and, with that one exception, completely absorbed in the workings of his own mind. He was almost pale, the sunburn having faded during these weeks of leisure and seclusion to an even tan, and there were definite charcoal lines beneath his narrowed eyes.

"I came in to tell you something. I want you not to be scared by finding out suddenly that that man is staying in the house. I've got him shut up down my way. I don't reckon he'll last long; last stages of alcoholism. And I've sent for a male nurse."

"But," Sally could not restrain her protest, "but why do you have to have that horrible creature here? You certainly can afford to send him to some institution, some hospital. He isn't ... he can't be ... anyone you ever cared for?"

"Perhaps I owe him something. Perhaps there was a time when he was a different sort of guy than he is now."

"Perhaps," said Sally, for it was obvious that he was manufacturing his reasons, "perhaps you have to give him what he asks. Perhaps you are afraid of him."

To this Vincent said nothing for a considerable time, his poker face betrayed neither feeling nor thought. Ignoring her suggestion, he asked, "Why did you come downstairs again last night?"

Sally's face, as far removed as possible from that of a professional gambler, gave its owner away in a great blush and a wide sensitive look.

"I . . . I was . . . I came down to ask your pardon, Vincent, for my rudeness. It wasn't really as bad as it sounded."

"You mean the way you laughed at me when I asked you to be my wife."

"Yes. It was because I was so terribly surprised."

"Surprised that I love you. I thought you knew that."

"Of course I didn't know. You've not been at all like a lover. You've insulted me and humiliated me a dozen times, and hurt me a lot. And I really believed that you loathed me and wanted to get even with me."

"That's because I told you that first afternoon when Marr left us alone together, that I had the whip hand and meant to use it?"

"Well, is that the sort of speech that makes a girl think that a man is falling in love with her?"

"It might be, if you were a girl who'd had more experience with men. If a man's scared to kiss a woman he usually wants to beat her up."

"I've had quite a lot of experience, thank you, but not with that sort of man."

"Not with any *man* at all."

"You're not so darn old, Vincent."

"I started living about fifteen years sooner than most. My father was too busy giving himself hard liquor to care about giving me anything in the way of protection. He left my mother and me when I was about eight. I guess she was a woman you'd be justified in leaving. She . . ." Here he avoided Sally's eyes, the only emotional use he ever made of those slaty orbs. "Well, I guess she did the best she could at that. Least said, soonest mended. I reckon she must be dead or, reading about me in the papers, she'd have turned up by now."

"Didn't she love you at all, Vincent?"

"No. Looking back, I reckon she loathed me . . . like you do. She left me in the hands of a 'motherly' female, one of those big fat oozy ones that pat you on the head when someone's looking and biff you where it hurts most when they get you to themselves. I quit her in about four months. When I wasn't being licked I was being starved. That's when I began to grow up. From that time on I've been on my own; lost track of both my parents."

"What wicked people!"

He shrugged. "There's a plenty like them."

"No. No, there aren't, Vincent. Most mothers care."

"Look what your mother . . . fine woman as she is . . . look what she did to you."

"But, Vincent, she meant to do everything for me. Everything."

"And what she did do is to bring you up with the training of an heiress and see you turned into my . . . *housekeeper*."

Sally half rose, sat down and put her hands over her face.

"I know you're not going to marry me," said Vincent. He paused but she did not say a word, just let fall her hands, showing her strained, unhappy face. "But what are we going to do?"

"We?"

"Sure. I can't let this story go on growing up against you. I got to fix it someways."

"For one thing, Vincent, you should get rid of Manchi. It was Manchi that started the talk."

Vincent's eyes went to slits and his lips almost disappeared.

"Sebastian Manchi. Well, I never heard that firing a man kept his tongue quiet. But there may be other ways of silencing him."

Sally felt a certain thrill of satisfied rage.

"I seem," said Vincent, "to have got me all tied up."

Sally, remembering how he was "tied up" with her

mother and herself, resented this complaint which he had made before.

"It wasn't Caleb Winter's will that tied you up with people like that horrible old man, Vincent. It was things you did in your own past. It must be because you are afraid of him that you can't feel safe letting him stay anywhere but in your own house. He might talk . . . tell your secrets?"

Vincent came to the desk, rested one fist upon it and leaning down his whole weight lowered his head until his eyes were level with and close to hers. She kept herself from drawing back.

"I am not being blackmailed by that man, Sally. I am not afraid of him."

"But you are afraid of somebody named 'Fred,' and you'd be in a mess if somebody named 'Tinka' was alive."

Vincent sprang back, his whole face changed. It was astonishing to see how from a light mask his youthful face assumed an iron one.

"How, in Heaven's name . . ." He looked about him rapidly, came to her and gripped one of her wrists. "Where'd you see Fred? Tell me. Tell me quick."

Sally laughed and looked down at his grasping fingers, her eyebrows raised, until he let her go, thrust the hand into his pocket and said quietly, "O.K. Tell me then."

"I never have seen Fred nor Tinka."

"She's dead. There was never any doubt about that. He killed her."

After considering this statement, Sally went on. "You thought that I was Tinka when I was sitting beside your bed at Grassways Inn. You were delirious. You told me you were afraid of Fred. Was it Fred you thought you heard outside the windows the night you turned out the lights and sent me upstairs, or was it this horrid old tramp you've taken into your home?"

"It wasn't anyone," said Vincent. "At least if it was I didn't get him. But I thought it might be Fred. Some night," he added gloomily, "it's going to be Fred . . . which is one good reason why you'd better marry me. Because you're likely to be a widow any day and then you'll come into Winter's money and Jessica's house and be free to marry a . . . Virginian gentleman."

"Why," asked Sally in a voice steadied by an effort of her will for she was afraid of him again, "why are you so sure this Fred will come to kill you? What did you do to him?"

"I got him sent up."

"For murdering a woman?"

"For murdering his wife. She had quit him, was living with a guy called Kiddy Bray. Fred killed her but the evidence pointed to Kid. They were both friends of mine, see?"

Sally said in the voice of a schoolmarm, "You ought to choose your friends more carefully."

Vincent first stared at her and then produced his quick short sound of amusement. "Sure. You're right at that. But Fred was a great guy. He was one of the rum runners I was boat mechanic for. I reckon I told you once. And he was sure the best pal I ever did have, or any other guy. The other boy, Kiddy . . . well, did you ever get a stray dog or a homeless kid wished onto you? That was the way it was with me and Kiddy Bray. He hadn't the makings of a man, wasn't any good really but he was like a kid . . . sort of got round you. He trusted me like I was his dad. So when they got him for the killing, see? they'd have given him the chair or hanging. For the way evidence looked it was a lot worse case for Kiddy than it would be for Fred. Anyway, Bray couldn't have took it. He'd have gone nuts. Nor a man couldn't have stood to see him hanged. Besides knowing he wasn't guilty. He was innocent and he wouldn't ever have hurt a girl like Tinka, or any other girl. And I was the only witness that could get him off. I . . . well, I had to squeal on Fred."

Vincent's face was twisted out of its mask of composure.

"I never did get to see Fred after the sentence. I guess he never would let me get to see him. But I got word all right that he was going to get me as soon as he got let out."

"Why wasn't he sent up for life?"

"Because the way it happened he kind of got a

break. It looked like it might have been that he'd meant to hit her in self-defence . . . sort of."

"You mean, harder than he intended . . . killing her accidentally?"

"Sort of like that. Besides, she was his wife, see? and had quit him for the other guy. Mitigating circumstances. Kiddy would have got hanging sure."

Sally sat there, considering the young man in the lurid light of his association with Fred's history.

"And Fred is out?"

"Yes, ma'am. I got word about six months ago and I was kind of keeping me pretty dark. Then come this will of Winter's and I got dragged out into the limelight. Of course I never was known as Obadiah Crewe so I'm kind of counting on being alibied. But that will wear out. Fred will get on to me sooner or later. It ain't that I mind so much more than you'd naturally mind being shot."

"It's that you mind being shot by Fred," said Sally, "before you have a chance to tell him why you had to witness against him . . . a chance to explain . . . to make him understand?"

"That's it. You surely can read a man's mind, Sally."

Sally smiled in a sphinx-like fashion and gave him, through her eyelashes, a rather guilty look. She was feeling like a "gunman's moll" and rather liking it, though prickles ran up and down her spine.

Vincent said, coming closer, "So, if you marry me, you likely wouldn't be troubled by me very long."

"I am not going to marry you."

He took this in silence and without any change of countenance. But half a minute later, he took her roughly into his arms and forced his lips upon her. Then, holding her in a grip that felt like the arms of an Iron Man, he spoke to her so closely that she felt the movement of his speech.

"You don't rightly know how I love you. You laughed at me for speaking poetry. But that's not because I feel just poetical. I'm hungry for you. I been close to starved a hundred times but that feeling's not anything for sharpness and . . . and hurt . . . to this. Don't try to hit me. I won't kiss you again. It was just to show you. No, it was because I couldn't help it. I touched your lips once. I didn't sleep for the feel and the taste of them. Don't you run away from me . . . if I let you go."

"I am afraid of you," she whispered.

"You got no cause to be. I know how to keep myself in hand. Now that I am sure you won't ever give in to me, I can kill out the hunger I've got."

"You won't want me in your house."

"If you leave it, I swear . . ." he tightened his painful grip, "I swear I'll leave it too. I'll sell it . . . burn it down."

He let her go, stepping far back and holding down his hands. From the door she looked at him. Her eyes were cold, shining, wet.

"It's only for my mother's sake that I must stay. It's only until I can think of something else to do, of somewhere else to go."

"By Judas, why do you hate me like that?"

"It isn't hating . . . it's that I'm afraid. Something inside of me has a . . . a terrible fear of you. It's creatures like that old man, I think, that come out of nowhere and fasten themselves on you. A murderer, prowling about to shoot you. There's a . . . a sort of blackness behind you like a storm coming up. You seem to be threatening . . . I suppose you'd say—because it feels like that—threatening something inside of me . . . my heart feels scared."

At that, Vincent's eyes opened to the width of his delirium and when she had got herself well out of his sight, a mile away, running to the river, seeking the shelter of the trees . . . she could still see this sudden transformation, this changeling Vincent, evoked she could not tell by what sentence she had used for his repulsion.

Chapter 17

Having gone through the uncomfortable ceremony of explanation, apology and amends, Robin Ashe became a senior of Yale University and returned, thinner, whiter and more silent than ever before in his life, to his Virginian home. Aunt Heather was about to move her household and its dependents to The Beach and thither Robin and his father were to follow their women when the summer cottage should be thoroughly prepared. Ronald saw no disturbing symptoms of brokenheartedness in the conduct of his son, who drove normally about the county visiting whatever friends still braved the heat, golfing, dancing, flirting and, to all appearances, enjoying his vacation.

There came a day, however, when Robin's car forsook its habitual channels of entrance and of exit, and, turning east from Hanbury, ran smoothly about the curves of a certain lane and in at a farm gate that opened upon the grounds of Crewe House. By this inconspicuous side entrance Robin betook himself to the front door at which he rang and presently asked of bobbing, smiling, almost dimpling Charles if he might see Miss Keyne.

It was late afternoon and the sun back of Robin and of the trees in the long drive was red as a Valentine's heart transfixed by Cupid's arrow. Charles, facing the glow of nature and of the young man's face, blinked.

"Just step in, suh. If you don't object I'll jes' take and put you into the lie-bury. Seems like Mr. Crewe been havin' visitors of consequence in the big room himself."

"The library will suit me," smiled Robin. Beneath his correct exterior of summer sport togs, his heart was la-

145

boring and plunging. As he followed Charles down the hall from which he had been, two months before, so abruptly dismissed, he glanced about admiringly and with a certain pang, at the background of a great house which should have been the background of the girl who had picked him up at the St. Charles Hotel in Baltimore.

The library made him open his eyes, it was so beautiful. He stood first at the window looking across the bed of tulips, now changed to pansies, heliotrope and sweet alyssum, towards the woods, then, restless with suspense, turned to the portrait of Jessica, whom he did not recognize as the cause of his young uncle's past transgression. He had always known the story ... had heard it whispered that Heather Gayle's husband had loved Jessica Crewe, had been on the eve of divorcing Heather in order to marry her, when he had, so opportunely for the marital conventions, been killed in a motor accident; that, shortly after the catastrophe, Jessica had married Caleb Winter. But the young woman in this portrait looked, Robin thought, gay and mocking, not in the least like his notion of a tragic heroine.

He heard a step, his pulses jumped, the heavy old door opened. There stood Crewe's young "housekeeper by courtesy," as white as her sheer sleeveless frock, and looked at him with her proud great eyes.

Robin came to meet her and took the hand she mechanically held out but did not hold it longer than for the conventional quick pressure, it was so cold. He looked about for a chair. She sat down in a casual sidelong fashion and Robin took his own place more stiffly on the blue brocaded sofa, first offering and lighting for her a cigarette. He looked up through the smoke of his own presently and smiled in his mother's fashion.

."I was scared you wouldn't see me."

"There is no reason why I should be unwilling to see you," Sally returned, smoking rapidly and holding her eyelids open wide.

"In your letter, you said," he closed his own charming dark eyes that had so haunted her, and recited, " 'I don't want to see you again. I don't want to think of you. I am going to forget you.' " Robin opened his eyes. To her astonishment, they were bright with laughter.

"I wasn't being funny," said Sally.

"I know you weren't. That's why I thought you wouldn't see me. I was going to park on your doorstep and keep on ringing until tomorrow morning."

"I am seeing you. But please don't keep me any longer than is necessary. I am only just a little curious to know what you have come to say."

Robin threw away his cigarette and leaned forward earnestly. His narrow and straight-featured face was serious enough and had turned pale.

"I've come to say that I haven't got your will power, Sally. I can't forget you . . . and God knows I've tried."

"Go back and try harder," said Sally and half rose.

But he came so close to her that to avoid his touch she reseated herself abruptly and looked up at him, pushing back her tawny hair with a quick nervous hand.

"That's what I won't do. I want you and I mean to have you, Sally. You're so darn beautiful, darling. I never did see a girl with such eyes, such a mouth. I've thought and thought about them. Listen to me, honey. You've got a plenty of common sense, I reckon. Here's what you and I have got to do."

She waited, trying not to melt to his beauty and his young sweet eagerness. His face was so changeful, so fluent after that of Vincent's.

"Relax now, will you? Don't perch as though you meant to dash out of the window as quick as I get out of your way."

Sally relaxed and resumed her air of nonchalant smoking.

After a piercing look to be sure she meant to stay, Robin went to and fro across the room a couple of times and returned to his forward-leaning pose on the love seat.

"I want to marry you at once," said Robin.

Sally straightened, color flashed up into her face. She held herself with her free hand tightly down on the chair. Her lips fell apart but she would not speak. She held her breath. Her eyes were as golden as her hair.

"I've not a cent of my own. Neither have my parents. We're all completely dependent on my aunt, Heather Gayle. You get all that?"

"Yes, Robin."

"I thought I could wangle out of Aunt Heather, who's really fond of me, the money she is providing for my education here and in France, so's we could marry and live on that until I was making enough to take care of us. Well, Dad and Mother told me that was *out* ... definitely. I couldn't get a copper to be married on. And that was before they'd heard this story ..." For the first time his look and voice faltered. But he kept resolutely on. This was a speech, long prepared, not to be interrupted by his own confusion, not even by her deep flush.

"That story, of course, about you and Obadiah Crewe."

"Which you believed," Sally whispered. "Which you believed."

"That story put a finish to any chance of financial help from Auntie. If I chucked my college career, as I'd planned to do, I'd be up against it. Flat. None of the family would help me. I'd be about ready for relief. So, though I've racked my brains and lain awake nights I can't see any way out for us ..."

Sally took the hand that had been holding to the chair and laid it over her eyes.

"But, Robin, I don't understand. Do ... you ... still believe? Or did my letter put me right again?"

He went straight on, his bright eyes narrowed in the effort he was making to stick to his planned speech, not by any interruption to be diverted from it.

"I can't see any way out for us but just one way, Sally. And it's perfect. If you don't agree with me that it shows I'm a man of genius, I'll be disappointed in you." He smiled, mischievous and endearing, again rid himself of his cigarette, put down a slim long hand on each small arm of her chair and went on in the wheedling southern voice, his curly head set coaxingly on one side. She could not help but look up into his eyes and, having looked, could not help but smile herself, widely and boyishly ... for Sally's smile was much less feminine than Robin's.

"Aunt Heather won't give me a cent to marry you

on, Sally darling, but she gives me for my education, and will be giving me for years, a lot more than enough for two. Why, I keep my own car. I can have everything I want. And there's nothing I want, nothing I've ever wanted or ever will want, honey, like I want you. So, why not this? You come with me and we get married quietly somewhere and next term you live in lodgings not too far from New Haven. Do you get it, Sally?"

Sally's smile had disappeared. Her eyes had a bewildered look and showed all their variegated freckles of blue and brown and green. She drew away and pushed herself free from the barrier of his body and his arms. She tried to think.

"You mean ... marry me secretly and I'd live there on your aunt's money? She thinking all the time that she was using it for you ... and ... nobody would know I was your wife ... and that might go on for years ... until you had finished your education and were able to make some money of your own?"

"Well, you see, honey, even if the family would stand for it and pay our bills, which they won't, I don't reckon the faculty would let me keep a wife while I was in the university."

"But suppose they ... the boys ... the faculty ... found out about us ... me?"

Robin shrugged, his whole face lighted with wickedness and charm, and he put his arm about her warmly. "What's the difference?" he said. "That doesn't prove anything."

"You mean they'd think ... I was ... I was ..."

"Tell me this, honey. Wouldn't you rather be taken for my mistress than for Obadiah Crewe's housekeeper by courtesy?"

Sally then looked beyond him and saw that the man himself, Obadiah Vincent Crewe, had stepped during this last speech of Robin's from an open door quietly into the room.

Sally thought, "He is going to kill Robin," and she spoke quickly without any conscious thought.

"But, you see, Robin, I won't be taken for Mr. Crewe's 'housekeeper-by-courtesy' because I am going to become his wife."

She saw the change in Vincent's eyes first and next in Robin's.

Vincent spoke. "I am sorry you didn't hear me come in."

Robin turned to him a furious countenance. "I am sorry," Vincent began again, "that I heard what you just said. I was going to beat you up and throw you out. I owe you a beating, but I reckon it would be more becoming to a gentleman to get my man to take you to the door. I rang for him. *You*, Manchi?"

Manchi must have been listening close at hand for he appeared from the room of Vincent's approach and now bowed and spoke smoothly. "Charles was called away, sir, for a moment, if you please."

"Very good. Will you please to show Mr. Ashe the way to leave my house and after you've seen him into his car and on his way down to the gate, come back here. I want to talk to you."

Robin, looking for the first time like a man who hated life rather than a boy who wheedled it, bowed and walked quickly out. He had not looked at Sally nor spoken a single word.

She thought, "Now I will never see Robin Ashe again."

Vincent stood perfectly still, a grey and narrow look fastened upon her, waiting for her to speak.

"I'm sorry, Vincent."

"I get you. You announced your engagement to put your boy friend in his place, that it?"

"I meant ... of course ... I mean that I will ..." Her breath forsook her.

"Marry me?"

In the smallest voice above a whisper that she had ever used, she said, "Yes, Vincent." And again they stood in perfect silence, Jessica Crewe looking down upon them with her gay mockery.

"O.K.," said Vincent roughly. "Now, get on out, will you? while I go over Monkey. He's coming back to take it and it will be plenty. Go on. Don't stand and fan your eyes at me like that. I'm not going to try to kiss you. I told you I was through with that."

"Perhaps," Sally murmured, red as fire, "perhaps now you don't want to marry me."

"Sure I want to marry you. That's fixed. Go on. Get out . . . quick!"

Sally heard Manchi's returning step, light and uneven, and, after one look of a hunted creature, darted to the open French window and fled through it, making havoc of pansies and heliotrope and sweet alyssum, and down the long darkening slopes of lawn and field. Alone she ran, a nymph no faun pursued, and reached the wood where on a feathery space of grass she threw herself down, plucked at the tender blades with a frantic hand, the while she laughed and cried and laughed and cried again.

For what sense could there be, what material for anything but tearful laughter, in a world where the villain rescues the maiden from insult by the hero, where the princess in the tower is driven to appeal to her dragon for his help, where her honor is insulted by Sir Percival and sheltered by him of the Red Laundes? Oh, Miss Mary darling, where is there any safe road at all?

So, brought back to that quiet upper room, sun-and-girl-filled, she heard the rational clear voice, advising her, "Don't expect miracles. Raptures. Don't look for demigods to adore or to be adored by. Don't, for pity's sake, envisage yourselves as young princesses in towers or sirens upon rocks. Be women . . . and please try to know and to like *men* as you will find them. Not the heroes and the demons of romance that the dream makers and reverie-producers tell you about . . ."

Sally questioned herself, Have I been expecting miracles and raptures, making demigods and villains out of mere men?

Chapter 18

Manchi came back into the room to find Winter's heir balanced in his boxer's pose, hands at his sides, beneath the portrait of Jessica. The valet looked him over critically: he did not as yet wear his gentleman's clothes quite like a gentleman, he still looked too robust, too energetic and too strong.

"You wished to speak to me, Mr. Crewe?"

The little yellow man stood with his pale bald head bent forward so that his face was grotesquely foreshortened and the prominent muddy eyes rolled up from their lower lids.

"It don't take much speaking," said Crewe. "I'm going to be married and you're . . . fired."

Manchi's spidery little fingers twitched, but for that, not a muscle moved.

"But, sir, by the terms of Mr. Winter's will . . ."

"I've looked into the legal aspects of your case. You'll get your legacy for life and I'll provide a reasonable sum besides for your living and personal expenses. That, Mr. Marr tells me, ought to make us quits. You talk too much, Monkey, and when you talk, you lie."

"I am not aware of having been indiscreet, sir."

"Maybe from now on you'll be more aware. Your job on Thursdays is to take folks about the house and to say your piece to them, it isn't to gossip about the members of the family. Get that?"

Manchi, by lifting his brows, made a play of corrugations across his head almost to its naked crown.

"I am at a loss, Mr. Crewe, to know what it was I said. I have no uneasy conscience. But, if I may so . . ."

"Say what you feel like getting off your chest."

152

"I don't believe, Mr. Crewe, that you will be willing, or, as it were, anxious to lose me, if you once come to realize what is my connection, my intimate acquaintanceship with the history and circumstances of your family, sir."

"Of my family?" Vincent's voice filled richly with astonishment while his face remained balanced and cold. "Who do you call my family?"

"I happen to know things, sir, that would make a difference to you, in respect to your situation here and, if I may say so, to your circumstances."

"Spit it out."

"Pardon me, sir." Manchi was at pains to close not only the door into the hall but that other by which Vincent had entered behind Robin Ashe, as well as the French window of Sally's flight. He then came back and stood close beside Vincent, rising on his toes to whisper.

"I have the evidence, sir, to prove that you are not the nephew of the first Mrs. Caleb Winter, of Miss Jessica that was."

Vincent drew away from the little whisperer, stared at him and then gave tongue to laughter.

"Why, you little yellow ape," he said when he was serious again, "are you trying to blackmail me or what?"

"You are not in fact the nephew of the first Mrs. Caleb Winter, as named in the will. Nor are you the son of Mrs. Winter's brother, Vincent Crewe, and of his wife. You are, in fact, the son of Miss Jessica Crewe by the gentleman she was about to marry if he had not been killed before obtaining his divorce. That gentleman's name, sir, was Mr. Peter Gayle. His widow lives hereabouts, sir."

Vincent, following Manchi's eyes, here turned himself about deliberately and looked up into the face of Jessica. His own was drained of color.

Back of him the honied whisper went on. "So you see, since by the terms of Mr. Winter's will, you are named as the 'nephew of my deceased wife, Jessica,' I imagine, sir, that the discovery of your true relationship to her would put you out of your inheritance."

Vincent still looked up at Jessica.

"Indeed, sir, Mr. Winter was well aware of this circumstance and worded his will very carefully so that you are his heir only as a nephew of his deceased wife. And he put into my hands, sir, the evidence, so that if you should turn out to be not just pre-cisely the sort of master we would approve, sir, for the Mansion, then I might produce the proofs and, in so doing, return the property into the possession of Mrs. Isabella, his widow."

Vincent then turned himself on his heel. He set his chin down against his tie and from that pose looked coolly into Manchi's face.

"What and where are your proofs, little man?"

"When Miss Jessica accepted Mr. Winter's offer of marriage, sir, she told him frankly that she was in ... trouble ... a trouble which she had hoped marriage with Mr. Peter would have cured. You, sir, if I may say so, were that trouble."

"You may well say so. Get on."

"Mr. Winter refused to give you the shelter of his name. Nevertheless, he was of a mind to wed this lady. So he arranged for her absence; he took her, in fact, after the wedding, for a long journey in South America, where, in a convent's nursing home, you were delivered and put into my hands. I took you, sir, to the brother of Miss Jessica who was married to a woman who was no credit to the family name. She and Vincent Crewe, sir, agreed for a consideration to call you their child and to bring you up as such. This bargain was arranged by Mr. Winter and kept faithfully by him as long as his wife's brother lived. And it was my duty to deliver the agreed sum to Mr. Vincent, returning from each delivery with a signed receipt. I have kept these receipts and also the paper of agreement drawn up between Mr. Winter and his brother-in-law in which, I assure you, the situation is definitely explained. It was the intention of Mr. Winter to hold this proof in his possession. It is all quite in order and available for the inspection of a law court. Mr. Winter was set upon that and gave the matter into my hands so ..."

"So that I would be left at your mercy, you little rat!

O.K. Fetch me the proofs. I want to see them with my own eyes."

Manchi rubbed his hands together and gave forth a musical note of amusement.

"Now, Mr. Vincent, sir, hardly! Hardly! You cannot expect me to produce them. I might not be willing to trust you," he added hastily as Vincent's body tightened. "Besides, sir, naturally, they are in safe deposit in a bank."

"Mr. Marr got them?"

"Indeed no, sir. Mr. Marr knows nothing of this . . . nothing."

Vincent's grey bright eyes bored into the shifty brain of the mulatto.

"You're a nigger," he said presently, "and I never knew a nigger yet that would trust anything valuable to a safe deposit box, if he could help it. I've a good notion, Monkey my friend, that those papers are in a box or a bag or a sack of some sort up in your bedroom across the passage from mine, and, since I have an automatic in my pocket, besides two fairly available hands and feet, I have also a notion that you are going to take me upstairs now into your room and that there you are going to find and to produce and to hand over to me the whole outfit . . . and no questions asked."

Half an hour later Vincent returned to the library holding a large manilla envelope. He looked as cool as ever but when, sitting down on the brocaded love seat, he opened his prize and took out for inspection the papers which it contained, his fingers were not altogether steady. He read them carefully, counted them, noting down their dates. He then less carefully returned them to the envelope.

He began to walk up and down the room, stopped to look across the fields towards the woods, where there was no flutter of a flying white dress. Two cigarettes he smoked to the last ash before he came again to the fireplace beneath Jessica Crewe's portrait. For as long as ten minutes he stared at the logs laid across the fire dogs and ready for a match. Then he lifted his right hand and placed it on the heavy gilded frame and looked up into the mocking and gallant little face.

"Lady," said Vincent who had no legal right to the

name of Crewe, "lady, I am prouder to be your illegitimate son by the man you loved than I ever was ashamed to be the son of that other woman." He stood straight, looked into the eyes of Jessica and his own he opened, full and warm and wide.

Chapter 19

Joseph Marr was well inured to the heat of a southern summer and rarely followed his clients north or to the coast until mid-July. But it was now nearing that season and he had already released his stenographer and seen his junior partner go. There was little to do in the stifling office but there at his desk the little old man sat, rustling his newspaper and continually readjusting his glasses upon a slippery nose, when Vincent Crewe presented himself at about ten o'clock of the morning after Sally's announcement of her intention to become his wife.

Marr had long before now become reconciled to the peculiar personality in control of Winter's estate and rose with some semblance of cordiality to greet him.

"Well, Mr. Crewe. Good day, sir. I hope you had no trouble with that wretched little mulatto." For, on the occasion of their last consultation, the subject had been the legal right of Manchi's persistent domain.

Vincent grinned, showing a fine blaze of teeth in his thinned and much less colorful countenance.

"He had a heap more trouble with me than either of us expected. But, before I tell you about that, I want to get some information, see?"

He sat down in his usual pose, bent forward, elbows on knees, cigarette in one hand.

"Has Mrs. Winter made a will?" he asked.

Marr was startled. It was not an inquiry he had any reason to expect. He replied, after a little pause of self-consultation, "Yes. Shortly after her illness. A very simple affair leaving to Sally everything of which she might die possessed."

Vincent squinted up through the veil of smoke.

"Good." After that he was silent for so long that Marr began to fidget and to clear his throat.

"This Manchi was a confidential sort of servant, I reckon, to old Winter?"

"Yes. Yes." Relieved at the break of silence, Marr became brightly conversational. "He seems to have had the trick of inspiring confidence in this most suspicious of his employers. He was first the servant of your grandfather, then of your father . . ."

"No, sir," Vincent drawled in a peculiar tone, "he wasn't ever the servant of my father."

"Pardon me, Mr. Crewe. It is something on which I have accurate information, first hand knowledge. Before Miss Jessica married, Manchi had just lost his job with your father, who had, unfortunately, offended his family by his marriage to your mother and gone with her to South America. Manchi remained at Crewe House and, after Miss Jessica's marriage, devoted his services to Mr. Winter."

"Nevertheless, sir," Vincent smiled, "he wasn't ever valet to my father. Mr. Marr, I've come upon a family secret . . . a family scandal, I guess you might say. Did you ever know that Miss Jessica, as you call her, had an affair with one of her neighbors?"

Marr started, blushed, took off his pince-nez. "Of course. Of course. The whole county knew of it. Peter Gayle was about to get his divorce in order to marry her. Our sympathies were very much, I fear, with the lovers, for Peter's legal wife was older than himself and a most difficult and tyrannical woman. Still is, as a matter of fact."

"You never guessed maybe," Vincent went on, "what was the cause of Jessica getting married to Winter so quick."

"Well . . . well . . . Winter had a great fortune."

"It wasn't Winter's fortune, Mr. Marr. It was Jessica's misfortune. She was going to have a child."

Marr jumped up, stood at his desk, quite pale.

"I'm sorry. I didn't mean to spring a shock on you. But the truth of the matter is, she was in trouble and that trouble, sir, was . . . me."

"Mr. Crewe, pardon me, but you are a man that

drinks pretty hard and the thermometer for the past few days . . ."

"No. I'm not crazy with heat or booze. I got the facts from Manchi, and by half killing the little yellow rat, I got the papers that prove he's right. Why old Winter trusted a Jamaican nigger, and a yellow one at that, with his secret, beats me."

"That kind often puts confidence in unlikely quarters. But tell me what Manchi said."

"That Winter left in his hands records of an agreement with Jessica's brother, Vincent Crewe, to bring up as his own son, a baby born to Jessica on her wedding trip with Winter in South America. It looks like Manchi went with them on that long honeymoon. When the kid was born in a convent nursing home, Manchi took it to Vincent Crewe and from then on delivered the sums agreed on in writing between Winter and Crewe and brought back the signed receipts. Here," said Vincent, producing the manilla envelope, "are the papers. Monkey may have held out some on me but that don't matter. Here are enough to cinch me."

"Cinch . . . you?" Marr was dazedly inspecting the contents of the envelope.

"Why yes, sir. If you remember Winter's will, it was kind of explicit about me being heir only as Jessica's nephew. Seems like he and Manchi had a sort of consultation before he got you to draw up that will and fixed it between them that if punishing the poor living wife brought into Crewe House a mighty undesirable citizen, Manchi had the power to oust him. If the little fool hadn't lost his head, he'd have taken a dismissal and carried his proofs to Mrs. Winter or to you. But he was physically scared of me and fear made him lose his nerve. Anyway I guess he'd have rather kept me on as owner under his thumb, see? But he spilled the beans and I picked 'em up. I admit I had to give him a sort of third degree but he was able to quit Crewe House last night and will likely bring suit against me for assault and battery."

Marr made no further comment, asked no further questions until he had carefully digested the papers in the envelope and carefully consulted a copy of Winter's will. After perhaps half an hour of this silent study and fifteen minutes of a sort of humming in his throat and desk-tapping—an interval which Vincent spent in patient smoking and an apparent study of the floor between his feet—Marr leaned back, sighed deeply and spoke.

"Mr. Crewe, sir, your honesty does you credit. I am rather at a loss to understand why, when you were to make the identical use of this evidence, you troubled yourself to use a third degree to get possession of them."

Vincent's color slowly rose.

"This may well mean," Marr continued with a certain sternness, "the loss of your recently acquired fortune."

"I tell you what," the young man spoke with surliness, "there was a little time in there when I wasn't, maybe, so sure I was going to show any particular honesty."

Marr hummed and hummed. "It is not easy to face such a loss, sir."

"That's how Monkey figured it out. He reckoned that I'd be scared to kick him out."

"This might well mean, sir ..." Marr took up his former phrase, but knowing that this young man seated before him was the child of Jessica and Peter Gayle had changed and softened the expression of the old man's eyes. He was, moreover, moved by an act of honor and of sacrifice, the more strongly, perhaps, by that blunt admittance of temptation. "I fear that it must mean that Mrs. Winter is the legal inheritor of the estate. That, of course, is merely an ex-cathedra opinion. You might make out a case for yourself. The phrasing is clear enough but a lawyer can create ambiguity, can pick flaws."

"I'm not going to hire me a lawyer. I'm going to get out. I've had three months of being a Virginian gentleman and that's about all, I reckon, I'm good for."

Marr rose. He leaned down on his hands and spoke with emphasis.

"If you will allow me to express my considered opinion, Mr. Vincent, it is to the effect that you have had about twenty-five years of being a Virginian gentleman and it is my hope that you will have at least twice as many more."

After a brief pause in which Vincent's face reachieved its copper hue, he muttered, "Look a here, will you go and tell the ladies? It'd come easier from you, I reckon."

"I would advise an intermediary period for your reconsideration ..." Crewe shook his head. "Well, sir, if you insist. But I should like to repeat ..."

"No. Not if it's got to do with me making a legal fight for the estate. That, sir, is definitely *out*."

And he stood up, looking, Marr saw with some amazement, younger, freer and more open of eye and face and smile than ever before in the lawyer's acquaintanceship with him.

So he went out of the office and down into the sultry street nor, in the interview with his lawyer, had he mentioned the fact of his recent matrimonial engagement to the young woman who was now again about to become the mistress of Crewe Mansion and of Caleb Winter's large estate.

This young woman had herself on the hot July morning taken definite action. She had breakfasted alone in bed but as soon as this meal was finished and she dressed, she went to her mother's bedside and sat down there, smiling and shaking her bright hair.

"Well, Mother, you'll probably be glad to hear that I have subdued the tyrant's rage."

"What do you mean, dear?"

Mrs. Winter's eyes doted on the fair tawny child, caressing her beauty of eyes and mouth and color, of proud breast and reed-like slenderness. Sometimes, to her mother, Sally seemed unbelievably perfect in her physical loveliness.

"And, Mother," here Sally laid a hand on either side of Mrs. Winter's face and bent her own bright countenance down until her lashes fairly tickled, "I've also subdued your rage and done something that's going to put you at your ease and make you feel as glad as anything. Can you guess, darling?"

"I can't. No. I can't ... you pretty thing!"

"I have promised, in the Victorian fashion, my hand to Mr. Vincent Crewe."

At that Mrs. Winter cried out harshly and loud and put her own free hand quickly to Sally's shoulder.

"Oh, Sally, Sally . . . is that true?"

"U-hum." The bright hair danced.

"But are you happy? Can you be? Only yesterday you said . . ."

"Yesterday is one thousand years ago, Mother. So much has happened to me since then, inside and out. Since yesterday I've grown up. You know that verse, 'When I was a child, I thought as a child . . .'?"

"But, darling, do you . . . have you been able to tell yourself . . . that you love Vincent?"

"That will be all right. I know it will be all right. If he is all you think he is . . . What was it?—Honest and humble and gentle . . . then the other will come."

She stood up, cool and smiling, as Vincent himself looked at that same moment in Marr's office, lifted her mother's sick hand, to fondle and kiss it and to put it down again.

"So I am 'still the Lady Claire' and you are no longer the ex-housekeeper, sweet, but the mother of the house. And Vincent thinks so highly of you, he will spoil you terribly. You'll have the best room and the best chair and you'll probably be carried downstairs by black slaves in a palanquin . . . is that the thing I mean? . . . and you will preside at table with me and Vincent at either hand."

"Hush. Hush. But what about the things that troubled you so? The secrets? The difference in his past life . . . ?"

Sally made her eyes huge and her mouth tiny, a face which no one could look at without laughter. "Oh, I shall get his secrets from him the way Beauty got the Beast's. And I'll educate him; he hasn't had a chance yet. And I think he will do for me the things I ask. There are a few things that he will have to do." Then she smiled again, spoke of an interview with the cook and went out.

For all her great eyes and her mobile face, Sally had never imagined that she had the makings of an actress. But no comedy queen with the proverbial heartache of the clown could have suffered a change of countenance more complete at the fall of a curtain than did Sally at the closing of her mother's door.

Sally's face within the door had been the face of happy, careless and triumphant girlhood; outside the door, it had become quite straight and set and pale and even almost stony. A resemblance to her mother emerged, a look, that is, of patience and a firm resignation to her own convinced will. For it is possible to rebel in secret against one's own decisions or to be to them utterly resigned. It was Sally's practical resignation to her promise of marriage that made her look like her mother when, a few minutes after closing the door, she sat down at her mother's work-desk. The world was an oyster to be opened for nourishment only. Sally was definitely done with her wistful search for pearls.

Chapter 20

Sally interviewed the cook, brought her accounts up to date and signed about a dozen checks. All the while she was thus occupied, she was aware of the silence of the house, conscious of a cramp within her bosom which was of suspense. At every instant she expected the sound of a step, unmistakable for its curious, brooding quickness, the opening of the door, the appearance of the man to whom she presently must fulfill her promise of herself. That he would hold her to this promise, she was convinced; in what manner he would hold her was as tormenting a question as could be put to a girl's inexperienced imagination. Besides this waiting, she was creepily aware of the presence above her in that house of the horrible old man. On her way to the office, she had passed his male nurse, a burly, soft-footed figure who carried trays.

That, thought Sally, cold of heart and finger tips, must be one of the conditions of her surrender. The old man must be taken to another home.

It was strange how her suspense grew, how it transformed itself to nervous fear, how, when a car passed her window and drew up before the house, it matured into a sort of panic so that she actually rose to lock her door and to stand close to it, breathing rapidly. She could not meet Vincent, could not look him in the eyes! It was Vincent's car driven by himself, but in an instant it repassed and she saw through a gap in the screening foliage that it still held Vincent under its steering wheel. Someone, however, had come into the house, had crossed the hall and was now beginning to mount the stairs. Sally opened the door in time to see little Joseph Marr's neat figure go trotting up out of her sight. She let out a caught breath, laughed in relieved self-mockery. "Mr. Marr to see Mother!", and rang for Charles in order to discuss with him a matter of silver cleaning.

Perhaps three quarters of an hour later, when she was again alone, a breathless little Early came running.

"Oh, Miss Sally, please, ma'am, your mother wants you quick as you can come."

"She's ill?"

"No, ma'am, Miss Sally. She just wants you to come mighty quick to 'scuss with her."

"Is Mr. Marr with her upstairs?"

"No, ma'am, Miss Sally, I let him out just now, ma'am."

Sally sped up the polished stair.

No sooner had she crossed her mother's threshold than she knew: realized, that is, a positive change, not only in her mother's condition of mind but in her own fate. Nothing but the dynamite of revolutionary tidings could have dragged Mrs. Winter up so high upon her bed, could have lit and opened her heavy-lidded eyes and sent into her face the pennants of life and victory. She stretched out her well hand to Sally.

"Darling, come here to me. Come quickly." With the reaching hand on Sally's arm, the eyes burning up, she went on with less of difficulty than she had spoken since her stroke, "You haven't talked to Vincent yet?"

"Talked to him? But, Mother, it was yesterday . . ."

"But not again since you were here with me after breakfast? Tell me, Sally, quickly please."

Sally laughed, her nerves in strong vibration.

"No, Mother. I've been minding my job. Vincent has been out."

"Thank Heaven! Now, sit down here. You must tell him as soon as he gets back that this marriage is quite impossible."

"Mother!"

"Yes. You told me that yesterday seemed to you a thousand years ago, that so much had happened to change you inside and out, that you had grown up . . ."

"I remember."

"Well, since you said that, another thousand years has gone by and everything in our world has changed.

We're free, daughter. We're free. No need to please or to subdue a tyrant. There's no tyrant. Caleb is dead. Vincent is out and, Sally, we are *in*."

Sally, her honey-colored freckles apparent, stared.

"Marr has been telling me that the will Caleb made was just a sort of trick. He punished me but not for life. He fixed that will so that Vincent can now be discounted, must, in fact, walk out of the house as only a few weeks ago he walked in."

"Wait a moment, Mother!" Sally prowled distractedly, found and lighted for herself a cigarette and, returning, stood close to the bed but would not come again within reach of that grasp which had given her a sensation of fear and of distaste.

"Now, tell me slowly please, just what Mr. Marr said. Was it something he knew all the time, to put us through a sort of test? I just can't understand. It sounds fantastic."

"It's no more fantastic than Caleb was himself. It's no more fantastic than a thousand other wills. The imagination of men and women about to die often takes a fantastic form to assert posthumous control of other people's lives. Caleb was very angry with me just before his death. And he had been angry before with another woman. His first wife deceived him as to her character and her estate. A child by another man. You see, the history of his hurt was repeated."

"Oh, Mother, please. Please."

Isabella Winter then did control her excitement and carefully enough described the discovery of Manchi's evidence and its result. All Sally's great eyes listened. Her face was now so pale that it seemed to have narrowed in its very bones.

"*He* took those papers, himself, to Mr. Marr?"

"Yes."

"He could have burned them."

"It was honest but, if he had not done so, he would have been guilty of a crime and, remember, that he could not be sure but that Manchi had held out on him some evidence sufficient to prove the case."

"Oh, Mother, don't . . . don't . . ."

"Don't what?"

"Don't belittle him. I've thought all this time that he was, perhaps, a sort of . . . criminal."

"You are a romanticist, Sally. It's time you learned some sort of moderation in your feelings. How to keep your head . . ."

"And now you think I should go to Vincent and say, *moderately*, 'I was going to marry you, Vincent, in order to share your inheritance and my mother was delighted with my choice, but now that I've got what I want, please consider yourself dismissed.' "

"You don't love him, Sally. You told me so yourself . . . not much more than two hours ago by that clock."

"And not long ago, you told me that he was so honest and gentle and humble a man that I could not fail to learn to love him."

"I did feel that. But, to be practical, darling, there was really nothing else sensible for either of us to feel. We were caught in a trap. We weren't free agents. I couldn't get away and, because you're my child and love me, neither could you. It was almost inevitable that you should accept this way out. Don't you see? And don't you see that this changes everything? You'd be a fool to marry the man."—Here Sally began to think of Robin Ashe with an increase of pallor and of confusion—". . . a man of whose past you know nothing, who is not one of your own sort, who has lived a life you can't understand and probably, if you did understand, could not forgive. He has secrets in his life . . . perhaps dangerous and shameful . . ."

"Oh, Mother, Mother, I can't believe it's you."

Mrs. Winter laughed shortly. "Because I quote you to yourself?"

Sally, seated now in a low chair beside the bed, had put down her face in both of her hands; her cigarette sent up its pensive smoke from the fingers across her hair so that she seemed to carry a pale slender plume. She was thinking against her will that it was no unreal or incredible mother who now used against her the very phrases she had so recently combatted. It was the real mother, the woman, who, with a lie in her mouth, had married Caleb for his money and had used that money in secret for a purpose he would not either have relished or approved. This was a woman who of a cer-

tainty opened her oyster with a shrewd eye to livelihood, who couldn't so much as imagine pearls.

"Go down now," cried Mrs. Winter, hearing the increasing hum of a motor in the driveway. "See Vincent
at once."

The pale girl raised her head and lifted her body
from the chair. She did not look at her mother.

"I will go down and talk to him," she said and nothing more, although her mother's eyes offered imperious
little question marks. Screwing out her cigarette, she
went out, like, Mrs. Winter thought irritably, a sulky
and obstinate young man constrained to obey unsympa-
thetic orders.

But in this comparison she was mistaken. Sally was
neither obstinate, sullen nor obedient. She did not go
down to talk to Vincent. After hovering in the upper
hall she charged down the back stairs, out of the side
door and through the hedged walks to the garage.
There she slid into the car she had not until this moment quite dared to call her own and sent her confused
and tormented self out into the droning day.

She could not do this thing to Vincent Crewe. She
had given him her word. If now he was no longer "the
rightful heir" nor she the "beggar born," it was none
the less distinctly "up to her" to marry her hobo and
make of him a Virginian gentleman. Could she now,
even if she had no promise to fulfill, turn to Robin
Ashe? Wincing, she recalled his face of a dismissed and
discredited lover. How queer it is, thought Sally, stopping her engine on a hilltop and gazing at her leafy,
breathless world, that just a few weeks ago I'd have sat
there in a tumult of joy and pride, feeling like a sort of
queen. Then I owned the county, my mother was to
give me parties, I was in love, ready to marry Robin
Ashe. And now ... and now ... it's all come back to
me ... all: the place, the fortune, the county, Robin
... precisely like something a genie does for you. And,
because of what's happened to me in between, I've got
no joy ... no joy. It's all gone, all spoiled. Her eyes
brimmed over. Mother ... I wanted to adore her, I
wanted to believe that she was a great, wronged lady.
And Robin ... he was to be my prince. That queer
copper-faced hobo I punished for his insolence ... ? She

set her teeth together, stepped on the gas and rushed down with the sensation of an eagle's flight. At the entrance to Crewe's farm lands she scared a couple of lovers out of the lane and, only after she had passed, recognized in the girl Nancy Brunn and in the man, that burly soft-footed nurse engaged by Vincent for his horrid protégé. It gave Sally a quick, small contraction of her nerves to know that that patient was untended at the moment, was locked perhaps into his mysterious privacy, brooding in a chair, that ashy blonde lock falling across his eyes. She forgot him when, as she climbed out at the front of the house, Vincent came down its steps to meet her.

He spoke to her jerkily, not meeting her eyes. And that, she thought, is because his face isn't a gambler's any more ... it's young. Open. All alive.

"Come with me somewhere, will you? I got to talk to you. Not in the house."

She led him into a hedged path, sweet with shade, pungent of box-perfume. It seemed, by contrast to the outer day, almost a channel of green water into which they moved. In a deep sudden cup where a circular stone bench had been placed beside a little pool they stopped. Sally sat down; he stood beside her, looking into the quiet bright water. Goldfish glittered and turned.

"Have you seen your mother? Has Marr talked to you? Do you know what's up?"

"Yes, Vincent."

"Well?" He gave her a quick sidelong glance and smiled like an unwilling boy. "That means I'm back where I belong. I'm sure a hobo and just as soon as I can sign off, I'm on my way."

She stood up, came to him, laid a hand on each of his arms; his own hands were pocketed. "Vincent, look at me. What do you think we are ... my mother and I?"

But he did not look at her, stood quite still in her grasp. His strength was in her hands, a curious sensation.

"I've seen your mother," he said slowly and flushed crimson.

Sally felt the warmth of her own shame flood up, break across her brow. Her hair grew damp.

"Oh, Vincent, she's old, she's sick. She's had a wretched life. But, you know, with me it's different. I'm not like Mother."

"She's packed me off, like you did when I got picked up by George into the front seat of your limousine. Say, it's yours again now."

"It's ... *ours*. Do you suppose I'm going back on my promise now, after what you have done for us? Do you think I don't understand how ... how straight a thing it was?"

He did then slowly turn his eyes. They looked as they had looked at Grassways Inn when he had been in his delirium.

"And that means," he asked her, holding himself steady as a post, "just ... *what?*"

"It means that I am going to marry you, and I keep my promises. I am, I hope, as honorable as you."

He startled her, shaking her off with violence.

"I'll have nothing to do with that. I'm not your policeman ... won't drag your honor into court. Here's your promise back, along with your estate and your money and your horses and your motor cars and your big house up yonder. And you can take your honor and big cold eyes and your mouth of an angry duchess." He choked. "And keep them for ... your Virginian gentleman."

"Thank you, Vincent." Sally spoke sweetly and smoothly, her eyes upon his. "Thank you. You do set me free, with both hands, don't you?"

There they stood, face to face, very close, both colorless, both shaking. Past his pride the passion in him spoke and pleaded.

Sally did not in the least know what she felt. The confused pity, the anger, the sense of lost power, of growing incomprehensible pain, drove across her brain and body like a stormy mist. There were a thousand half-words, half-cries snatching at her throat, huddling her tongue. None was ever spoken. Into their cup of tortured silence there came the sound of a slow, shuffling step. Turning together, pulling apart, they saw on his way to join them the figure of the horrible old man. He was dressed in a flannel robe, wore leather slippers, was clean and combed. He moved across the gravel, clawing at his skirts.

Vincent pushed Sally aside and back.

"Go round through the garden to the house. Don't pass him. Don't stop here. Go to your mother, Sally. Go into her room and stay with her and, mind you, *lock the door*."

Chapter 21

After Sally, looking to her mother's eyes like a sullen and obstinate young thing constrained to obedience, had swung out of the room, Isabella Winter was at leisure to rejoice. At first Marr's news had scared her nerves, sending an unbearable tumult along the unaccustomed channels of hope and pride. She feared ... she feared ... disaster, a fluke, a trap, some legal fumble, she feared that Sally had in some way committed her future to Vincent, had sworn to him some unbreakable young oath, had even been quickly conjured to the marriage altar. This match which had been her heart's desire was now her heart's despair.

It was not until this instant of solitude and of relief from her most pressing apprehension that she was able to indulge herself in a renovating glow. Not in any of the moments of her life, not even when, oppressed by her secret, she had stood before the clergyman with Caleb Winter, had she been in a mood of self-congratulation so profound. The end ... the end ... How did the old phrase go? The end crowns all. Her cleverness and patience had now their late and sure reward. Since the report years ago in San Francisco of her first husband's death, a blow softened to her by Jack Keyne's long absence and neglect, she had fought her battle single-handed and now was able to taste again, sweet as Olympian nectar, the fruit of her lifelong campaigning. Now she would be well. Now she would be strong. The vivid happy plans came back to consciousness as though taken out unwrapped, from some old chest. Parties to introduce her pretty Sally to the county. Satisfied vanity ... gorged pride. A match. All that she had suffered for the child rewarded, healed.

Sitting up, straight and strong against her pillows, forgetful of the partial helplessness of her disease, staring without conscious sight at the opposite door, she saw only Sally: Sally exquisite in New York frocks, Sally with orchids and roses, Sally at play, her skirt swinging to the turn of a golf stroke or to the quick dart of a tennis court, Sally dancing under the crystal lights of Crewe House, Sally at the piano, on horseback, radiant with love, in satin and lace, a bride. Sally a mother. The free corner of Isabella's mouth bent to an almost difficult smile of tenderness. The vicarious tenderness of "grandmamma." Now there would be time to be simply and with heart's ease, a happy old woman.

During the last part of this reverie Mrs. Winter had been bothered in one corner of her attention by a sound. Some trailing branch seemed to brush at irregular intervals across a rough surface, an odd noise for such a still hot day. It was like a gardener brushing at fallen leaves with a broom of twigs. No ... it was like a dragging step. She remembered that the end of the passage that led to her own and to the servants' quarters was carpeted in a long central strip of fibrous stuff. Someone very slowly and with pauses was shuffling his feet along this ropy surface. No one in the house, thought Isabella Winter, had a step like that. There was no other invalid, no old woman, no cripple, no old man. The step was definitely nearing. Isabella put out her hand to touch the bell. It hung on a cord close to her pillow but must have slipped away during the activity of her triumphant interviews with Marr and Sally, for she could not reach it. She was about to lift her voice to call for Zona when that door was slowly opened from the hall.

There was entering a figure utterly unaccountable to her. It was dressed from neck to slippered feet in a flannel dressing gown, roped about the waist; its head hanging forward was covered with grey-blonde disordered hair, one lock of which fell down across the tufted, ashy brows. The hands of the figure moved along its body, travelling almost to the knees and up again, without cessation. The eyes, once very large and of mixed coloring, were rheumy and shifted restlessly.

They reached her once—forsook her, moved slowly back, the while their owner advanced with the dragging step across her floor.

When he had reached the foot of her bed, Isabella spoke.

"Jack Keyne . . . you're dead," she said, a thick and guttural assertion of a fact.

He peered as though his sight had been impaired. He smiled doubtfully. "That you, Isa? I thought I'd find you. They left the door unlocked. The pill he gives me didn't work . . . I spit it out while he wasn't looking. Yes . . . I guess you thought I was dead all right. I worked it pretty carefully. I'd got tied up to another woman, Isa, down in Rio. I didn't want you to have any doubts but that I was killed in that scrap. I'd no money to go through the divorce courts or to pay lawyers. The other girl was pretty . . . young. I knew you'd land on your feet anywhere, anyhow." He laughed with a thick sound of phlegm in his throat, transferring the motion of his hands to the foot of her bedstead, his eyes still peering at her, as though they were searching through a deepening dusk. "I didn't reckon you'd marry another man. That's where you fooled me. But I never meant to plague you. I saw in the papers how your rich husband had died and I thought he'd left you a pile and that you'd kind of take care of me. My girl down there was dead. Things weren't so good with me. I'd got the liquor habit and it had got me plenty. The doctors told me I wasn't good for long. Thought I'd just drop in and ask you to make me comfortable for the time that was left. I wasn't going to hurt or scare you any. I wasn't going to tell the world you'd got one husband living while you married your second man. No, I wasn't. I swear to God, it wasn't in my mind." He began to cry and to rub his face with one hand the while the other began again to pluck at his gown.

Isabella spoke in the same throaty and undirected voice.

"How did you get here? Why do you look like this?"

"The fellow that got your money away from you . . ." Keyne lowered his voice warily, "he got to see me first and, after I'd told him my story he wanted to keep you from the trouble of knowing what you did, marrying Winter. He gave me money to keep me quiet. When I came back again he gave me more. Last time I came ... it was at night and I was sick ... he put me to bed here in the house. I guess he was scared to have me anywheres about, thinking I'd tell someone ... but, Isa, I wouldn't do that. No, sir ... though I let him think I might ... needing money so bad. I've been put down the hall back there ... a man in charge of me. The dope he gives me didn't work ... I wanted to see you, Isa, just once. I wanted to ask you about that little yellow-headed kid of ours. You ought to understand."

Oh, Sally ... Sally ... Sally! Grief and anger and fear surged up into the helpless woman's throat. She struggled to raise herself, to deny and to command her ghost. There was no faintest memory in her at that instant of young first love. Only horror and hatred and guilty dread. If she had had a weapon she might have killed him. Perhaps he saw the will to his obliteration and to his eternal silence in her dark face for he began to whimper again and to shake, looking about him for help or refuge. Shuffling sidelong to the door, he went out and closed it upon Isabella's frantic search for the lost bell.

When Sally came, fifteen minutes later, and bent over her she was able to move her head a little and to speak once.

"I think God punishes," she said. "Tell Vincent that I have no rights."

It was that confession of surrender, that effort at honor and at truth that killed her body and set free her soul: a confession and an effort completely uncomprehended by the shocked young ears that were the only ones to hear.

"My darling Sally," wrote Mary Culpepper with less than her usual restraint. "It nearly breaks my heart not to be able to be with you during these sad days. But now that you are sorrowfully released from your duty to your mother, you must come to me and stay with me until the road ahead of you is clear again. I shall expect a wire at once saying that you are on your way.

"I have had an extraordinary visitor. He an-

nounced himself to me, a most romantic youth.
His name is Robin Ashe. What he wanted of me
was that I should go down and speak to his family
on your behalf. I was to be" ... Miss Mary sur-
prisingly reverted to her far western idiom, for she
was born on a Montana cattle ranch ... "a recommendation on the hoof! This Robin, I gathered,
has offended you and desires with all his heart
reconciliation and forgiveness. I am to use my
good offices. He did not explain the nature of his
offence but most romantically beguiled me with his
smile and his penitence. I told him, Sally, that I
could do nothing for him, as man or lover, until I
had talked him over with you. So that must be one
of our subjects. His description of your employer
at Crewe House gave me, I must admit, a bad
night. I was urged to believe, against every conviction I have of your character, that you are to be
forced into a marriage with a gangster. I was able
to keep my head above the drowning waters of my
maternal instincts only by telling myself that this
was the report of a lover on a possible rival. Or is
Mr. Crewe a rival? I know you will understand
that I don't mean to force your confidence but it
may possibly be a relief or a clarification to
present your case to a sympathetic ear. I am
sorry, Sally, that the road that lay before you and
looked so smooth and flowery that afternoon we
talked together should have turned out such a
steep and thorny trail. But come to me and let's
see what can be done about it.

"And let me, if I can, comfort you! You are
brave, I know, and you are so dreadfully alone.
Your foster mother, 'Miss Mary.' "

This letter brought Sally down into the hall of Crewe
House one sad week later, dressed for traveling.
George Elmer had brought her roadster, now indisputa-
bly her own, up before the door. She was to drive herself.

At the sound of her descent and of an uncertain
summons, "Vincent, are you anywhere about?" Vincent
came out from the workroom. He carried, to her

amazement, a pistol in his hand and coming up to her held it out.

"I want you, please, to carry this with you in your car. I don't hold much for ladies travelling alone, even though you are going to make it before dark. If you don't mind, you'll just stick this into your car, to please me, understand?"

He was looking at her steadily, his eyes seeming to take no part in the process of his spoken thoughts. She took the heavy weapon in her hand and held it down against her dress.

"I don't think I shall need it, but thank you, Vincent. Will you write to me?"

"I'll stay on here," he said, "until my old man gets through with his dying. I give him not more than a dozen days of it, perhaps fewer."

And he envisaged a grave, nameless, not far from Isabella Winter's. Perhaps, he thought grimly, they, two, will reach for reconciliation through the dust. But of these thoughts nothing was visible or audible to the black-clad girl, standing with her gun.

She took courage for a question.

"You can't tell me who he is?"

"It wouldn't do anything for you or for me if I did tell you."

"Nor why you have to shelter him?"

"It is an old debt, Sally. I owe him something." His eyes were fixed changelessly upon her face so that it flushed above its pathetic draperies. Sally's slender blondness was accentuated by mourning. She looked dramatic, too colorful for anything but the pages of a romance.

"And, after his death . . . then?"

"I'll sign off with Marr and take the road."

"Vincent, you must wait."

"Waiting's not my line. What for?"

"You'll be needed. This thing can't be settled so simply out of court."

"Sure it can, me not disputing anything."

"But I feel, and so, I think, does Mr. Marr, that you *ought* to dispute. I want to go halves with you, Vincent."

Vincent grinned. "So Marr told me. I've no mind to be your pensioner."

"It wouldn't be like that. Oh, what's the use?" She turned from him with a gesture of anger. "You're a stubborn, ignorant boy. I can't help you or reason with you or even," she managed to let laughter spring into her great eyes, "or even . . . marry you."

At that his eyes did for half an instant flicker.

"Nor marry me," he said and in the same breath and the identical colorless tone, "Good-bye."

She changed her gun from right hand to left and shook his, murmuring one sentence, "I'll be with Miss Culpepper if you want me, Vincent," and knew too late that she had been cruel for his face looked like a reflection of itself in shaken water and he repeated, "If I want you . . ." and let her go, turning himself quickly back into the shelter of her workroom. There, as she drove herself past the windows, she fancied that he was bent above her desk as she had once been bent by grieving, an arm stretched out . . . did it too lie across the poem he had "read out" to her?

> *"With thy clear keen joyaunce*
> *Languor cannot be*
> *Shadow of annoyance*
> *Never came near thee . . .*
> *Thou lovest but ne'er knew love's sad satiety."*

Sally left Crewe House which would presently be her own, with a sensation of final and irrevocable farewell. She would never see it again . . . that was the conviction . . . nor him . . . nor him.

Chapter 22

In that charming upstairs sitting room of Miss Mary Culpepper's summer privacy, the shutters were drawn to mitigate the heat and a light breeze stirred the shadowed curtains pleasantly. Miss Mary at her desk looked up at frequent intervals from a letter for she was puzzled and perhaps alarmed by the entire immobility of her young guest. Sally in one of the chintz chairs sat as still as plaster, her eyes lowered as though they were studying her own hands. Miss Mary wrote: "I promised you this letter, otherwise I should have shirked it. Sally Keyne has been with me now for ten days and we have talked about you. You ought, my dear boy, I do think, to have been the husband for Sally. I wish you had been. But ... and I fear by your own mismanagement, you've prevented that. She is the right girl, wrongly wooed. I am sorry, although, I am sure, that you will be as happy, perhaps even happier, with another sort of wife. I rather like, myself, your pragmatism and I don't object to the deft and light-fingered fashion with which you will handle your life, but that is inimical to Sally's nature. She is intense, single-minded, proud ... no compromiser. A woman, I'm afraid, for whom no bread will always be preferable to half a loaf. I am sure you won't take my word for it, Robin Ashe, but I want you to give up Sally here and now and forever. It will spare you something to take the surgical short cut now to your eventual recovery. Sally, I feel it in my bones, won't stay with me very long. If you mean to hear her final decision from her own lips, you must run down ... or up ... here quickly. Something is smouldering in her ..."

At this point the girl, whose smouldering had been

hidden for an hour behind her lowered lids, stood up, came swiftly forward, dropped to her knees beside Miss Mary. The eyes she lifted, thought the startled school mistress, seemed to be fashioned only for the expression of ardor and astonishment.

"Darling," said Sally, "will you be furious with me, or hurt, or disgusted if I leave you right away now ... this morning?"

"Leave me?" Miss Mary put down her blotter across her instantly fulfilled prophecy. "To go where?"

"To go," said Sally, "home; to Crewe House."

"To Crewe House?"

"Yes. If I drive fast I can make Hanbury before dark. Of course I won't stay at the house. I'll stop at Grassways Inn and I won't see Vincent until tomorrow morning. There's something that frightens me, something that I forgot."

"Something that frightens you? Something that you forgot? Is Vincent still at Crewe House?"

"He hasn't written to me. He was waiting for the old man to die. And I'm afraid." She stood up and moved vaguely towards the door. "I'm so afraid he'll just disappear."

"You can't be content, perhaps, with a long distance telephone call?"

Sally smiled.

"No, Miss Mary darling. Even if he isn't there, I can't be content."

Miss Mary looked and looked. Then she announced slowly, "Ah ... I imagine that you will have to go."

The highway, as she turned into it from the narrower lanes of Maryland, looked to Sally both beautiful and safe. She had chosen a shorter route than that one followed by George Elmer on their trip south in May and now sped along the regular groove of eastern American migration, the blue mountains folding themselves with the convolutions of lolling dragons along her horizons. As she went, the salient features of her recent experience began to emerge like misted mountain heads in a landscape long familiar, now altered by the viewpoint of a traveller in the air. Her mother ... Robin ... Vincent. Robin ... Vincent. Vincent ... Vincent.

She remembered that this road, safe and beautiful as

it had also appeared on the day of her first home-coming had, nevertheless, been for her a road of doubt and tears. She had actually drawn back into her corner of the limousine to cry. Now, the soft warm air in her face, lifting her hair, rushing at her nostrils, she could find not even the impulse to a tear in her heart. That organ felt big enough to encompass all the dangers and the sorrows of any road. She sat spear straight behind her wheel and her eyes were consumers of the fuel for happiness. If only they could consume the miles!

She would not stop for lunch. It seemed important to reach the neighborhood of Crewe House before dark, even if she were not actually to enter it before tomorrow morning. Ten mornings ago she had left Vincent, she had allowed him to turn that shaken face of his and to go with it into that dreadful little sombre room. Oh, no, into that dear, safe and secret room, where she would find him again tomorrow.

Sally, the horsewoman, spoke to her car, "Get on, you! Don't you know I've got to be with Vincent . . ." and like the Red Queen to lagging Alice, "Faster, faster, faster!" Fortunately the travel southward in August is light. Nevertheless, even without delay or accident, she saw the evening star stand in a clear amber air as she swung down the long wooded slopes that led into her valley. Already the groves of oak and ash, of pine and maple and hickory, massed in their pale tilted fields, had the shadowed sameness of night. Lights of the farms and the big houses were equally tranquil in the same democracy of homes at dusk. It was dark by the time she reached that corner where, from the highway, a dirt road led in to Crewe House. Sally was driving slowly now. It was past ten o'clock. Vincent, if he were still in this part of the world, would not yet be in bed. Would he be pacing the breathless, empty rooms, with all his shutters and his curtains closed? She thought, "I won't be able to eat or sleep until I know whether he's gone or . . . waiting." But she did not want him to know until morning that she had returned. Morning is safe, thought Sally, and sane and manageable. What a woman says to a man in broad daylight he cannot easily discount. She would call upon him in the morning . . . yes. But, all the while, her roadster was slipping quietly along the leafy winding lane. It would be better for sound sleep if she knew that Vincent would surely be there tomorrow to receive her visit. And, if he were not there . . . she could sleep at Crewe House. Her heart paled and stilled. How dreadful then would be the summer night.

At a leaf-hidden fence she ran her car to cover and stopped, climbing down into a slender path which she was able to distinguish more by memory than eyesight, having followed it a dozen times in her escapes from Crewe House when that had been her most unhappy prison. Now, with hand out and a foot careful of stones and ruts and roots, she felt her way into and out of a copse and, more boldly across an open field. There . . . as she stepped into the woods again and descended a steep slope, was the branch. She jumped it, just touching water. She felt the coolness splash against her ankle. Then up the steeper slope beyond—the trees were terribly thick—to come out, triumphant, in the open grass below the gardens. Now she could see the house. There were lights sticking slim fingers through the shutter slats. The stars and the sky were clear above the long dark roofs and chimney tops. She could hear a negro singing.

Her haste and night-entangled effort had made her wet and her breath was quick. Suspense kept fumbling at her pulses. She went more slowly, trying to compose herself. She reached the nearest gate in the long brick wall, pushed it open and went through. Her foot, expecting gravel, struck against something soft, heavy and warm.

Sally bent low and groped with her hands and with her startled eyes. It was the body of a little dog, Vincent's little yellow dog, that had followed him home from Hanbury and been his companion ever since. Sally lit a match which burned itself out in the still air while she examined the little creature. He had been killed—only a short time ago he was so warm and soft —killed instantly by a heavy blow on his head. Sally stood up, as her match went out, and felt cold. A little dog runs out barking at the sound of a footstep in the garden walk. The bark is cut to silence. The footstep goes on, forsaking the gravel for the soundless turf, goes on without further warning given, towards the house . . .

First she started to run and throw herself between Vincent and Fred's bullet. Then a second thought drove her back towards her car as rapidly as though that difficult path were lighted by a noon sun, splashing into the branch, stumbling, balancing, recovering, until she had her hand on Vincent's gun, the one he had forced upon her as she said good-bye. With this to make her interference effectual—if all interference did not come too late—she returned to the garden path with its pathetic futile little sentinel.

Sally stepped like a ghost towards the French window of the library and found, standing the while in the sweet alyssum, that it was mercifully unlocked. She sat down and took off both her shoes. Inside the house, all the lights were burning brightly and there was no sound. Very distantly she could hear the negro singing. She stepped along the old polished floors and came into the hall. It was as still a house as the Sleeping Palace. Perhaps she had come too late. Perhaps her fear was based on a false premise . . . a whiff of cigarette smoke gave evidence to her attentive nostrils and led her, as light of foot as an apparition, to the office door. Light shone here across the threshold but no sound came from inside. Something, however, gave her the chill of an excessive fear. Her cold hand pressed and, infinitely careful, turned the knob.

What she did, as the door opened, was purely instinctive. She could never remember what the quick series of her action was. She stood inside, her back against the closed door, her gun was steady and her voice of vibrant silver wires had finished its clear speech.

"Don't move. I've got you. Lift up your hands . . . high . . . high . . . above your head."

The man, whose presence she had more divined than recognized, did stand up slowly from his chair. He had been tilted back against the wall close beside Mrs. Winter's desk; the floor about him was strewn with cigarette butts. On the desk top within his reach but not within a reach as quick as her intuition had allowed him, lay his gun. Opposite the watcher, and his attentive, patient smoking, Vincent slumped down in the desk chair. He was tied into it by a short rope which strained his elbows together behind the back. A handkerchief was tied across his mouth. He was instantly recognizable as a man in a dead faint. Sally moved across the floor and stood beside him to face his visitor. She cautiously drew towards her the gun on the desk and dropped it into the pocket of her light coat. It sagged down heavily. She kept telling herself, "Don't think you're safe. You can't be safe as long as he is here. Don't let anything . . . not any cry or oath or terror . . . make you take your eyes by one flicker from his face, nor move the direction of your gun. He has a wise cold look . . . he can beat you at this gun game easily. Oh, Miss Mary, Miss Mary" . . . and she did not in the least realize how quaint was the summons of the little spinster school mistress for support in this emergency, "please help me to be strong and calm, to keep my head."

So her mind was busy while her tongue spoke, addressing the deadly danger to which eye and hand were steadily directed.

"I know who you are," she was saying. "I recognize your face. Vincent described you to me that night at Grassways Inn. Your name is Fred. You killed your wife. You are just out of prison and you have come to kill Vincent. I know all about you."

"You surely do know a lot," the man spoke in that voice Vincent had said was "so low that you have to listen close to understand what he is saying to you." "But you have got me wrong. I came in here to save Vincent from Fred. Lady," he hissed this out with sudden and desperate urgency, "you better look behind you quick."

Every nerve in Sally's body jerked but her body itself stood still. She saw how he gathered himself for a spring and how he now relaxed.

"You're pretty good," he admitted, "for an amateur with guns."

"I thought when I first looked at him," she said, going on in the even high tone of her first speech, "that you had killed him already. But, if you had, you wouldn't still be here. The dog barked at you and you stopped him barking and Vincent went out and you hit him on the head and stunned him and carried him here to kill at your leisure. You want him to know who it is that killed him. And he wanted more than anything in the world, I think, to tell you first how he was forced to give that evidence."

The face described by Vincent in his delirium ... "a narrow face ... like a knife ... black eyes, close together, a long nose ..." changed subtly during that last sentence of Sally's speech which by its tone seemed to be addressed to herself. Perhaps the change of her auditor's expression brought her again to full awareness for she spoke more sharply.

"I am going to wait five minutes and then, if Vincent has not come to, I'll telephone for the police."

But she had hardly finished this announcement when Vincent stirred and groaned, and tried to lift his head.

Moving her left hand only she clumsily undid the handkerchief that kept him from speech.

"What happened?" muttered Vincent. His eyes under the scattered red hair were dazed, slowly gathering evidence of reality. "You, Fred?" He turned then as far as he could, wrenching at his bound arms, and looked at Sally. After closing his eyes tight and opening them again, he whispered her name, *"Sally!"*

She said superfluously, "I have come back."

Then his voice cleared and his face became its old, resolute and cool gambler's countenance. "Get that penknife over there near the ink well ... it's open. And cut this rope. But don't move your eyes or your gun, see? Take your time. There's no hurry. Where's his gun?"

"In my left pocket."

"Good. We're safe if you don't lose your head. We've got the night before us. Go easy now. No hurry. Just feel for the knife."

She felt for and found it, felt sideways for his rope and inserted the small sharp blade. It was slow work, like the gnawing of a little mouse ... she sighed in nervous agony. Strand slipped from strand ... then a quick jerk on his part and he was abruptly free. After moving his numb muscles and rubbing his arms he took the gun from her pocket, saw that it was loaded and sat straight, facing his man.

"I want you to get out of here now, Sally."

"Oh, no . . . no."

"Go out and wait until I call for you, please. Pronto."

Sally said, "I will sit out there in the hall close to the telephone and, if I hear or see anything that scares me, I'll send for the police."

"O.K.," said Vincent. "Shut this door."

She obeyed him.

She went to the alcove beneath the stairs and sat down beside the telephone there, her gun on her knees. She had no breath nor strength—and a white mist kept travelling across her eyes. She could hear the sound of Vincent's voice, a friendly and earnest voice, pleading, reasoning. Of Fred's answers not a sound. The voice went on and stopped, went on and stopped again. She head the sound of a chair pushed quickly back, a short exclamation. Silence. And that silence lasted.

She waited. Her heart which had grown steady jumped and shook. That watchdog in her subconscious mind, the one that had warned her truthfully that the insolent tramp who had stood waiting for her one evening at the foot of the stairs had dangerous power over her heart, now painted for her nerves a picture as terrible as truth. Fred had gone. Vincent was dead. It had not been a gunshot . . . it had been a sudden blow like the one that had killed the little honest dog. Vincent now lay across the desk, his head down on his arms. She had been a fool to leave him, half dazed and weak and bewildered! This was the end.

She stood up, not knowing that she was shaken by sobs, and went as though dragged by a cruel invisible hand and opened the door. She saw no one. A curtain came towards her gently, blown by summer night air from an open window. She called faintly, and would have fallen if Vincent himself had not caught her in his arms. He had come to her from the window. She held him back, putting her hands on either side of his thin, colorless face.

"No, Vincent, no."

"What brought you back? Oh, forget about Fred. He's gone. It's all right. I made him understand. *What brought you back?*"

"I came back to tell you that I love you dreadfully and that you have got to marry me."

Then she began to laugh, because her own statement sounded so bald and commonplace, as though she had said, "I had forgotten my umbrella."

"Listen to me," she cried, still forcing him to keep his mouth from hers. "You must let me speak. I don't care about your past or your secrets."

"There's only one I've got to keep from you. That's buried with the poor old man. It's not my own."

"I don't care. I don't care. You can be anything ... a hobo or a tramp or an ex-rum runner or just one of the unemployed.

> " *'If you are but a beggar born*
> *And I, said she, the rightful heir*
> *We two will wed tomorrow morn . . .'* "

But that was as far as his patience would allow her young lips to move in any action so superfluous to their desires, as speech.

Katherine Newlin Burt and her husband, Struthers, have both been successful writers. Mrs. Burt is best known for her romances, many of which have appeared in *The Ladies' Home Journal* and other magazines. Some of the colorful settings in Mrs. Burt's novels come from having lived in several sections of the country—from Philadelphia and North Carolina to a log cabin and ranch in Wyoming, which the family owns, in part, to this day.

A former fiction editor of *The Ladies' Home Journal,* Mrs. Burt is the mother of two children. She has written eight books published by New American Library, including THE LADY IN THE TOWER, LOST ISOBEL, and THE BRANDING IRON.

More Romance from SIGNET

☐ **THE LORDSHIP OF LOVE by Hermina Black.** Could she give her heart to one man, when she yearned for the arms of another . . . ? (#Y6650—$1.25)

☐ **VENETIAN INHERITANCE by Annette Eyre.** She was caught in the legacy of a forbidden love. . . . (#Q6524—95¢)

☐ **THE EVIL OF TIME by Evelyn Berckman.** Lovely Keith Elgin had come to The Castle determined to find the buried treasure. Could even John Ridge save her from the unleashed fury of the treasure's secret guardians . . . ? (#Q6427—95¢)

☐ **THE RAINBOW CHASERS (Condensed for Modern Readers) by Marion Naismith.** When David Lorimer appeared in the village, Louise found herself yearning for his love. But could she trust her heart to a man whose past was shrouded in mystery . . . ? (#T6330—75¢)

☐ **DANGEROUS MASQUERADE by Hermina Black.** It started as an amusing charade of love. But soon her happiness became the stake in a perilous game of hearts. (#Q6228—95¢)

THE NEW AMERICAN LIBRARY, INC.,
P.O. Box 999, Bergenfield, New Jersey 07621

Please send me the SIGNET BOOKS I have checked above. I am enclosing $_____(check or money order—no currency or C.O.D.'s). Please include the list price plus 25¢ a copy to cover handling and mailing costs. (Prices and numbers are subject to change without notice.)

Name_____

Address_____

City_____State_____Zip Code_____
Allow at least 3 weeks for delivery

Other SIGNET Romances You'll Enjoy Reading

Have You Read These Bestsellers from SIGNET?

☐ **FEAR OF FLYING by Erica Jong.** A dazzling uninhibited novel that exposes a woman's most intimate sexual feelings. . . . "A sexual frankness that belongs to and hilariously extends the tradition of **Catcher in the Rye** and **Portnoy's Complaint** . . . it has class and sass, brightness and bite."—John Updike, New Yorker
(#J6139—$1.95)

☐ **PENTIMENTO by Lillian Hellman.** Hollywood in the days of Sam Goldwyn . . . New York in the glittering times of Dorothy Parker and Tallulah Bankhead . . . a 30-year love affair with Dashiell Hammett, and a distinguished career as a playwright. "Exquisite . . . brilliantly finished . . . it will be a long time before we have another book of personal reminiscence as engaging as this one."— New York Times Book Review
(#J6091—$1.95)

☐ **CONUNDRUM by Jan Morris.** The incredible and moving story of a man who was transformed into a woman. . . . "Certainly the best first-hand account ever written by a traveler across the boundaries of sex."—Newsweek
(#W6413—$1.50)

☐ **SPINDRIFT by Jan Bryant Bartell.** The most terrifying book you will ever read! The story of a woman's discovery of a diabolical possession . . . of her fight against it and her eventual flight from it. "A spinechiller!" —Publishers Weekly
(#W6353—$1.50)

☐ **THE FRENCH LIEUTENANT'S WOMAN by John Fowles.** By the author of **The Collector** and **The Magus**, a haunting love story of the Victorian era. Over one year on the N.Y. Times Bestseller List and an international bestseller. "Filled with enchanting mysteries, charged with erotic possibilities . . ."—Christopher Lehmann-Haupt, N.Y. Times
(#E6484—$1.75)